NOT THE REAL MARILYN MONROE

Brian Swann

MADHAT PRESS
ASHEVILLE, NORTH CAROLINA

MadHat Press
MadHat Incorporated
PO Box 8364, Asheville, NC 28814

The Library of Congress has assigned
this edition a Control Number of
2017913116

ISBN 978-1-941196-57-1 (paperback)

Cover art: *La Femme au Cheval* (1912), Jean Metzinger
Cover design by Marc Vincenz
Book design by MadHat Press

www.MadHat-Press.com

First Printing

Not the Real
Marilyn Monroe

For Roberta, always

Table of Contents

I

II

I

Pol

Her mother had converted just before Temperance was born. She converted back soon after, but the name stuck. When her hormones were able to stand on their own two feet again, Temperance's mother began a search up various tangential family trees for venerable Sephardic respectability. She gave up when the family moved back to Long Island, where, at fourteen, Temperance became Nahtasha. At sixteen, she changed Schwartz to Flowerdew, and at twenty-one made it official.

In the same year that Temperance/Nahtasha was born, on a tropical beach in the Greater Antilles, an idyllic beach not yet backed with a Hilton hotel and only marred by a few dead dogs, human waste in various stages of decomposition, and some coconut husks shredded by wild pigs, Jim Flores's parents were busy engendering him. They were doing it with some dispatch before the searchlight swept over the sand in an irregular and futile attempt to detect smugglers of various interdicted materials, including arms. Since the government had recently been awarded a grant from Turtles International to buttonhole the locals supplementing their incomes with endangered turtle eggs, the searchlight served this purpose too. This beach had seen the prior conception of Jim's sister. Like the turtles, Jim's parents were creatures of habit. When presented at a later date with the infant Jaime, his sister gave him instant adoration and attention. So much so that once, at a much later date, when Jim complained that his shirt-collar was floppy, she grabbed the iron she was using and attempted to iron the collar while he was still wearing it. (She balanced worship with economy, however, only ironing his shirts above the elbow. When questioned, her answer was always the same: He always rolls up his sleeves anyway.) Warmhearted she was, and impulsive. Once she ironed a blouse while she was still wearing it.

One day, Jim's family left their island and sailed to Miami. From there they drove to New York in a truck borrowed from a distant relative. Eventually, Jim's father became a taxi-driver. He also took to beating his son from time to time. The one time he raised his hand to his daughter, Jim knocked him down and cursed him in English.

Jim left home at the start of his freshman year at City College and seldom returned. He cried at his father's funeral. He visited his mother in Queens once a week until her death, a year after his father's. His sister married an Air Force pilot and moved to England. She sent a card at Christmas until she divorced and remarried an engineer of Arab descent from Biloxi. His work took them both to live in one of the emirates in the Persian Gulf.

"Don't pay too much attention to the porch. It's nothing. Easily cleaned up." Jim had gone ahead to set things up, so this was the first time Nahtasha had seen the house they'd rented for the summer. It was the first time they'd rented anything together. They'd been living together for a year. The house belonged to an Italian professor and his wife. All around them had been eaten away by New Jersey's suburbia. But this ex-farm still retained woodland around it into which crowded all the bird and animal refugees. Nahtasha looked where she was instructed not to look. The porch was covered with excrement from every woodland and domestic beast and fowl. From inside, she heard her two lovebirds screech. "How did this happen?" she inquired mildly. Jim pushed aside a piece of curled fecal matter with the toe of his new Adidas. He'd just recently returned from one of his twice-daily runs. "Well, I put out food every night. And then I was away a couple of days—had to go to Philly on that Aetna case, I told you. So I left more food *out than usual." "What goes around comes around," she said. And thought: Typical anal retentive. Some even parcel it up and wall it into their houses. Still, he means well.*

Jim had brought his Exer-Bike with him. After an hour on it, he helped Nahtasha make dinner. Over dinner, he told her about the geese they were supposed to take care of. "Supposed?" "Yeah. Possums tunneled into the enclosure and decimated the family. The goose didn't have room to spread his wings and attack, head down, hissing, the way they do, you know. At least, that's what I read. The first night I was here, I heard this racket and went out, and I could see this possum keep jumping up at the goslings. It grabbed one and dragged it headfirst down its hole. Then it came back for the other." "You mean you just stood and watched?" "Well, not really. But by the time I got there, it was too late anyway." "You could at least have tried. You really hate birds!" "Oh, come on! Why would I feed them if I hated them?"

That night, Nahtasha couldn't sleep. She kept thinking of the baby geese being dragged down into the dark. The night noises seemed to come from everywhere, all around the house. Howler monkeys in the trees, hyenas in the uncut grasslands.

The lovebirds who'd greeted her arrival lasted a week. They were jolted into freedom when the weight of the cat who was sleeping on top of the cage broke the suspensory string. The cage crashed to the porch, and the door sprang open.

Jim is in the doorway. "So what's under the cloth?" he asks. But he knows. She pushes by him into the co-op apartment and puts down her bulky burden. Inside, something can be heard fluttering. Something starts to bang about inside. There's a squawk—and Jim goes ape. He flaps his elbows like a chicken and begins to clamber over the furniture. Then he dashes out the door and down the steps. Nahtasha picks up the cage and walks along the corridor. She knocks on a door.

5

*

"So what's in the cage?" I asked, after I'd calmed her down with a vanilla milkshake, a handful of baker's yeast stirred in, the way she liked it. She fetched up a sigh from the pit of her expansive blonde bosom. (How did I know it was blonde? Her hair was blonde as wheat, her skin like powdered milk. I imagined her bosom to be consistent with the rest of her. Draw no unwarranted conclusions.) "A conure." "A con— That's a kind of vulture! No wonder Jim—" "No. A *conure*. The kind that rolls over, pulls little carts, and does tricks. He cost five hundred dollars."

The next day, I knocked on her door. Jim was still at the office, doing whatever lawyers do. I inquired after the bird's health.

"He won't eat. I leave seeds and delicacies, but he just cowers in his cage. At the store, he was left alone, so he teamed up with a gang of cockatiels and became their boss. He nipped their ears and generally kept them in line. Here, the nearest thing to a bird is Jim, and he's still recovering from the last batch of birds I got. I think he's jealous. He stayed out late last night." I stirred some brewer's yeast into the vanilla milkshake I'd just made in her blender. I didn't care for the taste. I did it in solidarity. We drank together. Nahtasha was my friend. I didn't have many. "He's afraid for his books," I remarked. "He was jealous of those other two—the lovebirds." "Those *four*." It was a sore spot. In one of his compulsive vacuum-cleaning forays, Jim had sucked two babies up the pipe. Their first day out of the cage. They had blended too well with the carpet. I was grateful when Nahtasha ignored my tactless correction. "I called them by our names. But, to be fair, he did try to win their affection. They'd just never go to him. I guess threatening to pull out all their feathers can't have helped his case much. He's so beautiful." "Jim?" "No— Pol. I mean, yes, Jim too. But I was talking about Pol." "That's his name?" "Yes. Robinson Crusoe. On his desert isle. He did everything to make them go to him…. He's so beautiful—" "We've been there already." "Oh, yes. Anyway, these parrots are supposed to love bright colors. I remember Jim's cousin Julia had one, and it loved a colored wool tapestry she had on a wall. She was so fascinated with what the parrot was doing that she couldn't bring herself to stop it." "Stop it what? Do you have any nuts?" "No. Well, first it pulled out the yellow threads, each one, all over. It followed each yellow thread until there was no yellow thread anywhere. Then it pulled out all the green, following each thread obsessively. And then the other colors, one by one, one at a time. It took a week to denude the tapestry, until there was only the backing left. Oh—I just remembered! Some filberts in that dish on the side of Pol's cage." "I'll pass." "Pol's a Nansum conure. A cross. He may be sterile. He may be a she. It's impossible to tell." It was time to change the subject. Once Nahtasha took hold of a thread, she often hung on. She was wearing a white blouse, antique-looking, with embroidered birds of paradise spreading their multicolored tails all over it. I said: "I was walking back from the supermarket this morning when I saw this woman getting out of a taxi at Second and Twelfth." "You ought to find yourself another wife." Pause. "Jim keeps asking me to marry him, but I'm not ready. I've only known him two years." I ignored her. I never allowed myself to think of my wife. I said, "She'd just drained a bottle of fruit juice, and she smashed the bottle to the ground. But you should have seen her legs! Better than Betty Grable! And she wasn't wearing any stockings." "Do you think I should? He's such a perfectionist. He tries to make everything perfect." "Below zero with wind gusts. She had on blue high heels and a tiny pink mini that barely covered her dainty parts, and she kept tugging it down. She wore one of those thin black-leather jackets with tassels, cowboy-type—and that was it! I just had to follow. A fire engine blatted its siren, cars and trucks beat on their horns. A guy made a smacking noise with his lips, and she cursed him out. I crossed over to get a better look at her face— and she was beautiful! The looks of a film star. Completely out of it." I remembered my wife's legs, her ex-legs. I sipped the milkshake. What I tasted was the sour yeast. Nahtasha looked at me with blue eyes that seemed polished. "She probably *had* been a film star, and some man abused her. She took to drink, and then someone supplied her with drugs, and now she's on the streets. It happens all the time. Like this morning. I was going to work this morning, but it was so cold I thought, well, I never take the bus, but this morning I'll treat myself. I saw a group of three or four women standing on the corner, so I joined them. No bus came for quite a while, and when one did it stopped up the block. And then I realized."

Nahtasha reminded me of my mother. Softhearted. Wasted on my dad.

*

It's Saturday afternoon. Jim is on his Exer-Bike, trying to calculate matters right so he comes out "Elite" in his age group on the heart chart pinned to the wall. He has the fingers on his left hand pressed against his carotid artery. He has come to tolerate Pol because he does not shred his books or chew the edges of his art posters ragged. But he's not happy that Nahtasha won't clip the bird's wings. "It's unnatural," she'd replied. "And he'd only get underfoot, not to mention under the vacuum cleaner. He could get caught in your pedals as you go into your cycling trance." Jim is reading from a law journal propped up in the wire basket in front of him. Earphones are clamped to his head. He's working his way through the nineteenth century on tape. He's up to Tchaikovsky

(1840–1893) and is listening to the Overture Fantasy, "Romeo and Juliet"—"andante non tanto quasi moderato." *It has slowed his pedaling, but he hasn't noticed it yet. If he were to look up, he would see Pol standing in puzzlement over a crystal vase he's just knocked over in one of his uncontrolled, sweeping non-flights from his cage. Luckily, the vase fell behind the sofa. It will not be found for a while, since it is Nahtasha's turn to clean the apartment. She never cleans behind the sofa.*

He doesn't hear Nahtasha put the key in the lock and open the door. She has seen some talent for an upcoming revue (she is working for a theatrical agency) and found it wanting. Pol scrambles back to his cage and pulls himself up by his beak. Something makes Jim look up. "Oh," *he says.* "Have you been home long?" "Just got in." *Sweating, Jim dismounts.* "Anything good?" "If you call someone dressed like a mushroom, face covered with residual pimples, testing the stage by doing backflips on it good, then there was something good. Everybody is so predictable." "Like everybody in New York." *She has flopped down in a chair.* "Well, I did meet one original person recently. He's a clerk in 'California.' From Kansas." "I thought you said he's from California?" "'California,' the gourmet store. He's sweet. He comes into the store and says good morning to the cat. I say to him: Say good morning to the cheeses. Say good morning to the pies. Say good morning to the grapes." "Strikes me you're the only original person in New York." "He sold a girl a bruised apple. When he noticed, he apologized and offered to replace it. No, she says, I like bruised apples best. I know what you mean, he says." *She glances over to Pol. He is huddled in a corner of the cage.* "Do you know that before I take a shower each morning, I go to the fridge and take out a cold apple? Hot shower, cold apple." *She goes to the bathroom. After fifteen minutes, she returns wrapped in a towel.* "I want to go to Wyoming," *says Jim. He looks at the basil plant in the one window. She's kept it alive for months with pruning. They have basil with everything: eggs,* oatmeal, Jello. *"There's a tribe in Africa that slices off bits of their cows when they need meat." "Why Wyoming?" Nahtasha asks. "That trip I took to New Mexico last summer, for that conference, remember? I learned to ride. I like to ride." "Round and round in a circle?" "Up mountains." "Did you ever come down?" "I don't know what I did in a former existence to deserve such punishment. It must have been something terribly bad to get a wife who doesn't like to cook, doesn't like to clean, and won't go to the antique show with me. Who only wants to go to the bird store every weekend and handle the merchandise. I don't know what awful thing I did could justify this." "You probably went on and on like this." "What?" "You did the same thing to your first wife in your former existence, only worse, probably. This is your punishment for that. Put the clocks back an hour." "What did you say." "The clocks. Put them back an hour. Don't forget the kitchen." "What kitchen? What clocks? What house?" "Keep talking. I figure if I keep you talking long enough you'll forget about— Stop it! Pig! All men are pigs! I just put Stiff Stuff on my hair." "Boy, have I got some—" "Don't you dare say it! Don't you dare!"*

*

The big event had taken place at City Hall, among Hispanic women in bridal gowns. They did it without telling anybody. Jim, she told me later, had gone to see her father on Long Island and said, "I'm proud to announce that Nahtasha has agreed to marry me." Her father had said nothing. "So," she nudged him, "what do you think?" They'd timed the announcement for her birthday. "Elope," he said, and walked out. Her father had been an investigator of airplane crashes. Her mother said she had nothing against Spanish people. Then she burst out crying.

*

Jim was off again at some conference. He sure worked hard. Have to say that for him. I knew Nahtasha was feeling lonely, so I called to ask her out to dinner. I should have stayed in and cooked, but I cooked as well as I jogged. And I found this ad for a new health-food restaurant that said they used ten different varieties of brown or wild rice. I knocked on her door. It was ajar. "In here," she called. I could always defrost a burger when I got home. She came hobbling out of the bedroom. She reached up to a shelf and pulled down a paper doily. "Here." She took another and put it on her head. "Party time?" "Pol's taken to pooping on people's heads. Mostly guests. Sometimes mine and Jim's. Better be safe." I put it on. A kind of airy yarmulke. Nahtasha began to squirm. "Something wrong?" I inquired. "My pantyhose are too short," she hissed. "And I've just got my period." "I thought feminists weren't supposed to talk about such things." She retreated into the bedroom. Her doily floated to the floor, where it joined others. I followed and stood in the door. "Listen," she said, "at my age I'm boasting." Then she threw herself backward on the bed, legs in the air, trying to squirm deeper into her pantyhose. I backed out, sat down on the sofa, and watched Pol whetting his beak on the cuttlefish bone stuck through the bars of his cage, which was, as usual, open. I touched my doily, to make sure it was still there. Pol had grown quite large. After a short while, he stopped whetting, sat back on his heels on his perch, and went quiet. Suddenly, the sound of a vacuum cleaner filled the air.

*

I struck out fast with my right foot and ground my toe into the sidewalk, delicately. "Got it! Before it could escape to the gutter." "It's fun doing it," Nahtasha giggled. "Little ones." She had drunk too much rice wine. She kept giggling and hiccupping. "I know," I said, "I just can't for the life of me imagine a gorgeous woman doing that, especially through delicately scented silk underwear." "I'm not wearing delicately scented silk underwear. I'm wearing cotton. It's cold!" "Look! That one says, 'Nothing in Trunk.'" "And that one says, 'No radio under seat.'" "And that one says, '*Ceci n'est pas un voiture.*' No engine, no seats, no car, nothing." Nahtasha did a little skip. Everybody reminds you of somebody. "When I was a kid, my cousin made a bush from her father's drama whiskers and glue. She wore it to school but refused to go to gym class." "Is that the one who ironed her father's shirt collars while her father was wearing them?" "No. That's Jim. And his sister." "I'm out of breath. Let's sit on this wall." We did. "When I was a kid, I always wanted a dog, but my mother wouldn't let me have one. So I got a leash from somewhere and dragged it behind me. I'd turn now and then and talk to the dog, giving it instructions, you know. I'd even stop by hydrants and curbs. People would stop and say, 'My, what a cute little dog!' I felt they were real phonies...."

It wasn't late when we got back to our building. Nahtasha invited me back for a nightcap. I chose a Diet Coke. She handed me a doily and dropped another over the one already on her head. "I think Jim has someone else." I stopped scratching the parrot's head, to its relief. It shook its feathers. "Someone neater?" In truth, Nahtasha was something of a slob. The whole apartment right now, without Jim to tidy up, looked something like the bottom of a birdcage. Though Pol's was neater. "I'd hate to leave this apartment. Even though it's a bit dark, it's the nicest place I've ever lived in. It's a little island. And Jim's the nicest guy I've lived with, too, even though he drove his first wife nuts with his neatness. Literally. She had to have treatment. He's always cleaning. He's always busy." "He has a compulsion to better himself, to do a lot, to know a lot. He loves you. He always brings you back nice presents." Nahtasha turned on the radio and tuned it to some sixties songs. Somebody with a high-pitched voice and lots of yea-yeas. Then Elvis and "Are You Lonesome Tonight?" Pol was sitting on the saddle of Jim's Exer-Bike, having hauled himself up with beak and feet. He was making a strange, subdued, mechanical noise, something like the sound of the Exer-Bike when Jim rode it. I told Nahtasha that Pol was two or three times the size of any conure I'd ever seen. But she insisted. "Jim should go easy on that machine. He's convinced he's getting fat when there's not an ounce on him. He has a beautiful body. Unlike me. The doctor says he's in great shape—he goes once a month for a checkup! But he keeps telling him not to overdo it. I keep telling him he's pedaling away from death. And Pol keeps pooping on him. He can't get on his bike without Pol pooping on him. He's tried to keep his doilies on, with hairpins, but no go. He's starting to take it personally. He's getting pretty mad." She pulled up her legs and laid them across my lap. "Did I ever tell you of the time I lived in an SRO, near Grand?" I shook my head. She had. "It used to get so hot in the summer I had to sleep with my head in the fridge. My heels were pressed against the wall. The place was overrun with roaches, but a neighbor told me not to leave water around and they'd go away. This neighbor was a heavy-drinking prostitute with no front teeth. You never knew what she'd do next. One night, the fridge jumped with the banging on the door. 'Come on out here, Nahtasha, you bitch! You stinking two-bit bitch!' I opened my eyes. There was a wide gap under the door, and I could see a large pair of scuffed slippers sticking through. She'd done something like this before when she was doped up or loaded, but this time she was screaming that I'd slept with her boyfriend, who happened to be gay. 'Open the door, open the fuckin' door, you fat tart, or I'll kick it in!' When the door opened, she stood stock-still while I emptied a dish of water over her. Then she said, 'Oh!'

13

And then, 'Did I disturb you? Were you asleep?' and left." She swung her legs over and onto the floor. Nahtasha's legs weren't really like—hers. But the little bumps at the knees, on the inside … "Oh, the heat in that apartment was stifling! One day in July, my father arrived at my door. He always coughed, or whistled, or cleared his throat when he visited, in case I was with—you know. I was always his little girl. He carried an air conditioner up the five flights, and his face was white. He stayed a short while and left, after he set it up. I sat on my bed, the only furniture in the room, and turned the machine on. Bliss. I lay back and closed my eyes. Suddenly my nostrils filled with black smoke. I looked at the air conditioner. Not from there. Then there was a knock on my door. 'Come in,' I said. It was Joleen from down the hall. 'I've brought some beer,' she said. 'Jees, baby, it's cold in here!' Smoke was rolling around her, as if she was paying a visit from hell. I tried to keep down the panic in my voice. 'What's happening?' Joleen had opened the window and was squatting on the fire escape, twisting the tops off two beers. 'Fire. Here, this one's for you.' I went out with her and squeezed in beside her lanky, malnourished body. I could see other people above me calmly standing or sitting on the fire escape. Joleen's boyfriend walked in with one of his friends and sat on the bed. I asked them what was going on—I was calculating the odds of surviving a fifth-floor leap if the fire got this far. Smoke was coming out of the window below. He lay on the bed. 'The guy downstairs poured oil over everything and set it on fire.' Shocked, I asked why. 'Who knows, man? But he's the one with a wife and three kids, and they're all living in a room smaller than yours.' A fire engine pulled up below, and some firemen took their time getting out. That night never did cool off. My floor seemed to radiate with heat from below. My air conditioner had broken when Joleen opened the window onto the fire escape. I finally got to sleep when most people were waking up. I was sweating all over—I'd taken all my clothes off. But I didn't sleep for long. I felt little tickling motions over me, particularly between my breasts. I opened my eyes. Hundreds of roaches were sipping my sweat." "How long did you live in that place?" "A year. But the next morning I took the two completed chapters of my Master's thesis and threw them into the drowned and blackened room downstairs. I was writing on Strindberg's indebtedness to Siri von Essen."

Sometimes, I felt as if I was married to Nahtasha, but more as if I'd married my sister, or a particularly close cousin. Or a small force of nature. I'm sure, by the way the parrot looked at me sometimes, he was taking it all in. Or my wife, before—I never allow myself to think of her.

*

It was nice of them to invite me. I'd taken early retirement the year before. Twenty years in the New York school system should qualify you for veteran's benefits. The retirees and their families took an annual trip on the sloop *Clearwater.* I asked Nahtasha to come along with me. I asked Jim too, but he was convinced he had a hernia.

The first obstacles on board were garbage cans filled with ice and Coors beer. Someone handed Nahtasha a can. "I don't drink Coors," she told him. "The man's a fascist." I had no such scruples. I knew a Delaware Indian once, I told her, in Oklahoma. He told me that his brother-in-law was a Sioux, or something, who belonged to the Strong Bear Clan. This guy would *only* drink Coors because it came from bear country. They wade in and piss in the clear mountain streams, he said, streams they make Coors from. And that makes good medicine.

I didn't know too many of the teachers. Most of the people I'd known who'd taken early retirement had left New York as soon as they could. So I walked with Nahtasha to the

15

less-crowded side of the boat. "Look," she said, "Forbes's boat, *The Highlander,* all shiny and green! And a helicopter with it!" "Must be taking Liz Taylor back to Manhattan," I replied. Even this early, there were drunks leaning at various angles. "I think I'm leaving Jim," Nahtasha half-whispered. But before I could follow up, some woman buttonholed me, claiming we'd been colleagues in Tuxedo Park. I'd never even been to Tuxedo Park, but that didn't prevent her from telling me (ignoring Nahtasha) that she was trying to save Sterling Forest. Nahtasha had read about this, so she smiled at the woman, which was all the encouragement she needed. "I went out to interview an eighty-five-year-old man who'd written on the subject. I told you, I live in Tuxedo Park—there's only four digits to make a phone call. He was incredible. A real Renaissance man. A poet and inventor. He composed music to play on the calliope he'd built. Each weekend, he used to drive to Connecticut to drive a locomotive in a theme park. He invented an electric car and produced a plan for a monorail to run from San Francisco to New York, way before its time. He was a captain in the Merchant Marine, and he wrote a book on San Francisco. He was a real Renaissance man, and he's *completely* unknown." Nahtasha asked, "What's his name?" "I forget," the woman replied.

When the boat docked, we had to push our way onto the pier past members of the crew and another group that was waiting to board the vessel. Their fists were filled with Coors. I noticed for the first time that most of the crew members were wearing 'Boycott Coors' pins. We walked for a while through the Seaport. "I'm thinking of leaving Jim," Nahtasha said. "When will you be back?" "Forget it." They were still reconstructing the Seaport into a sanitized version of the nineteenth century. "Those little hill-towns in Italy, you know, like Siena ... They're not real," Nahtasha murmured. "Yeah,

I know what you mean. They have an unreal quality about them." "No. I mean they're deliberately planned—made up—like that. Look—you know Santa Fe?" "Yes." I didn't. "Well, it's like that. After the earthquake, the city fathers decided to reconstruct the place like a pueblo—or was that Santa Barbara? In any case, they have a pueblo six-story garage and a pueblo multi-storied hotel. Same with those Italian hill towns. They were originally haphazard rabbit warrens. They weren't even on hilltops. They moved them there. It was a decision made for the tourist trade." Would she move out of town if she left Jim? And where would that leave me? My life, for a moment, at any rate, felt as fake and precarious as the place we were walking through.

*

That night, I dreamed of my wife. I'd almost dreamed of her for some time, but this was her first full appearance. I had been dreaming of floating like a balloon over the countryside, visiting places I knew, and in the dream I had this dream. Or else I had awakened in the dark and was remembering…. I'm washing my shirt in the bathroom sink with Woolite, though I usually use Joy. "A wife is supposed to wash her husband's shirts," I call out. "I love this," she moans. "Ooo, Elvis!" She is doing her exercises in the bedroom. "Hillbilly sleazeball," I mutter. "I particularly love the talking bits. It's 'Are You Lonesome Tonight'?" "He must have stayed up all night learning the lyrics," I call out. She comes in, a light sweat on her naked body. "Look at my pubes." I turn my head. "They're *dyed!* A patch!" "I think I'll do them all." I take the nail-brush and scrub the collar. "They're bushy. Good. You've stopped clipping them. A woman's glory is her hair. My mother kept saying that. But if you're going to dye them, you should use black. A big black bush. A real woman." "I'm going to use green. A vegetable dye." "You'll give me food poisoning." She goes back into the bedroom, steps onto the New York Yellow Pages, heels over the edge, raises and lowers. She is working on her calves. Has been for years. The little bumps on the inside of her knees knock together gently. "Kiss me." I am almost halfway to the kitchen when I hear her. I think I'm putting Joy back, but when I look down I see I'm holding Woolite. "What?" "Kiss me. While I'm bouncing up and down." Up and down. Up and down. And the crab all the time is crawling up her calf.... I try to coordinate kisses with her ups, but I keep getting her chin or her forehead. She cracks up, and falls off. *Falls off. Falls off.* Falls off....

*

A man collapses in the street. Two people rush up, take him by his arms and legs onto the sidewalk, and lay him down in the snow. Someone leaps off his bicycle and tosses his coat over the man. A group gathers. The man goes into convulsions. His hat falls off, and a doily is revealed fixed to his curly black hair with pins. He is about forty, well dressed. Suddenly, like a resurrected corpse, he's on his feet, arms flailing, legs kicking out crazily. A young woman rushes into a bodega. "Call the police," she tells the guy selling Lotto tickets. "Sure, sure," he says, but does nothing. Minutes later, the woman runs back. "Did you call? You didn't call! Call!" She gallops out. "Sure, sure," says the man to himself. Then to a customer, "I call, too much damn paperwork after. Happen to me last time. The cops'll come anyways. They'll call a bus." "Bus?" queries the elderly Hispanic, pocketing his change. "Bus. Ambulance. Cops call an ambulance a bus. My bro's a cop—well, a transit cop. Same difference."

*

Nahtasha's mother, Ruthie, talked of sickness; she talked of colostomy bags. "My mother had a hernia," she told a woman who had come into the wrong room and sat down beside her. "But after the operation, we thought it had gone away. When I visited her in the hospital, she said, 'Lift my shirt, Ruthie, and tell me.' She had the body of a child, even after a lifetime of knives. At forty, they had to operate to crack off bone that had grown round her heart. Seventy pounds. She couldn't eat." "A hundred and twenty dollars of pills she left unused," Uncle Joe volunteered. Then he left again to walk up and down the corridor. "I remember her phone number," said Nahtasha's sister, Naomi. "458-9873. I remember every phone number. I can remember the phone number in your first apartment." She turned to her sister. "Yours, I mean. 442-7895." Joe returned. He had white hair, a polished red face with high Tatar cheekbones. He wore pants with, in addition to a crease down, a crease across. Apart from me, he was the only man. Nahtasha's father had refused to attend. "Looks like none of his people are coming," Joe remarked. "He had no family. I mean—" Nahtasha's voice trailed off.

At the brief service, the funeral parlor's old rabbi droned on. "He gets paid for this," Joe whispered to Nahtasha. When she didn't respond, he turned and made the same loud whisper to me. The skull cap kept slipping off the back of my skull. It felt funny. I wasn't sure I liked it. I was wishing I hadn't come. I half-listened as the rabbi went on about virtues and dribbled over us all sorts of Biblical homilies and various injunctions. It wasn't until he said that a good wife is worth rubies that I realized he must have picked up the wrong c.v. before the service or else he'd gotten what Nahtasha told him mixed up with a previous or a future subject. All the others seemed not to notice. Nahtasha was crying silently; her mother was napping; Joe, who was a bit deaf anyway, had never even met Jim. The rabbi went on about how the home was the center of her life, and how Esther gave to charities: how she was a loving wife to

Malachi and loving sister to—he couldn't read the name, so he coughed, and went on.

*

There were traffic jams at the cemetery. The limo door opened, and into the front seat jumped a middle-aged woman in black blazer, black dress, black stockings, black everything. She turned and talked through the opening in the glass partition. "I'm just hopping a ride. I can't get my car out. I'm the funeral director. We've got thirty funerals today." A jet screamed overhead on its way to Kennedy. In my ear, Joe whispered, "She's not Jewish." "Nor was Jim," said Nahtasha's mother, in a louder tone. "But don't say anything. I told them the name's Sephardic." At the family grave, the old rabbi, who had gone on ahead, gave directions. He read a prayer, and then he asked me to read one with him. Then he said, "Take a shovel." I stood there like an absent-minded gardener. The rabbi made a motion. I dug the thing into a pile of sandy dirt, then scattered it on top of the coffin. The gravesite of the family was wedged between two yew hedges. The roots of one had been exposed by the digging. Naomi wondered aloud if it was the right gravesite. She'd gotten the family names confused and couldn't read the names carved in marble on the gravestones at the rear. I hurled in shovelful after shovelful of reddish soil. The rabbi took the shovel from me and handed it to Joe. He attended all such funerals. He was something of an expert. While this was going on, I looked up and saw a guy getting into a fight with the chauffeur and funeral director. He wanted to drive by us on his way to another funeral, but we were blocking his way. He had a dead white eye and stroke-shivered face, dead white. There were streets crisscrossing the cemetery, with regular street signs on them. The man studied them for a while, then retreated to his car, cursing. When each person in our small group had tossed in a small shower of dirt, the four black gravediggers took over. We were about to climb back into the limo, but the rabbi restrained us. "It's a good thing to stay until all the earth is in," he said. So we all stayed. I looked at Nahtasha, whose face looked numb. The four black men worked hard, clambering over the mounds of soil, shoveling from all angles. When it was all in, the gravediggers hustled into their van and rushed off to another site. A Swissair jumbo jet bellowed like an ancient divinity over our heads. We got into the limo. It started to back down one of the narrow streets, careful to avoid a newly dug grave, two parties of attendant mourners, and their attendant limos. Our driver narrowly avoided another limo that had come the wrong way down the one-way street. The funeral director leaned into the front window and kissed the old rabbi, who was returning with us. "Thinks she's the director of Lincoln Center," said Nahtasha's mother. Joe kept eyeing the liquor cabinet beside the TV set. On the way home, the driver got lost among dug-up roads and dead-end streets. At one point, we found ourselves in the only green field left on western Long Island. And Joe wouldn't shut up. He recited stories from his career as a taxi-driver: "I never picked up blacks. I was afraid of getting mugged. The government has subsidized buses now, and *they* ride them to Jamaica to Bronx or Harlem. They don't need taxis." The Long Island towns slipped by, one running into the other: lawns, malls, houses, malls, houses. "I've had lots of famous people in my cab. Lots. They gave me their autograph. Sophie Tucker, who was very heavyset, got into my Checker cab once. One day, I saw Harry Truman. Without bodyguards. That was amazing. Just standing on the curb by the Plaza. So I U-turned and asked him for his autograph. Why? He said. Because I already have your wife and daughter, I said. Get out, he said. I did. Turn around, he said. I did. And he wrote his autograph on a piece of paper pressing on my back. Jack Dempsey had a high-pitched voice. I was also in *The Merv Griffin Show*—a passenger turned out to be the producer. I use Tide all the time, I told him. It keeps my hands clean. I thought I could josh my way to stardom, but it didn't work. Yeah, it's a dangerous job. Cops used to follow me and make me pull over. They wanted 'coffee money,' they said. They used to try to ride without paying...." He fell silent. "I'm glad they settled on plain pine." It was Joe again. "But that's what was right. As an Orthodox lady." I looked at him. Nobody else had been paying attention. He must have been talking about his daughter. Or his wife. Or his mother. I became aware that Nahtasha's sister was paying attention. She had an overlarge face, all pustules."I'm trying a hairstyle like Nahtasha's," she told me *sotto voce.* "It's also like a character my boyfriend Julio likes in *General Hospital.*" She told me her favorite food was sweet-and-sour pork. She said the doctor was happy with her weight. Then all fell silent.

*

That summer, I sold my small apartment and moved in with Nahtasha. Pol had taken to nibbling down the edges of Jim's books, making long, jagged strips from half an inch to two inches wide, which he (she?—we were now entertaining doubts as to gender) piled in his cage, like a nest. Nahtasha took some and made spirals or mobiles out of them with pins and Scotch tape and glue. She gave them to her friends. Sometimes, the words would form a crazy collage, a moving collage when stirred by air. Pol and Nahtasha: surrealists, bricoleurs. The library was rapidly reduced. Pol sometimes attacked the spirals and mobiles and rendered them to scraps and tatters, small as confetti, so the place looked as if a wedding had just taken place. After a while, Nahtasha gave up vacuuming.

The air-conditioners were having a hard time with a brutal

July, so I suggested we pack our bags, and the by-now large and talkative Pol, rent a car, and drive to the Adirondacks. I told Nahtasha about going in August to the Saratoga races with my father when I was a kid. She liked the idea. She'd been sluggish of late, complaining of various ailments and pains. So unlike her. She thought she needed a change.

We set off, Pol sitting on my shoulder as I drove and muttering the few obscenities I had taught him over Nahtasha's objections. "Shit, the war's over," was one my father had taught me, and I had passed it on to Pol. He repeated the phrase until we got on the Throughway. Now and then, Jim's voice would startle us and make Nahtasha cry. Pol interspersed his Exer-Bike and vacuum cleaner, very quietly, into my ear. Then he seemed to enjoy the scenery and shut up.

*

We were soon in Saratoga and in our bed-and-breakfast just outside town. By the time we'd settled down and taken a few side trips, the races had begun. In the first race week, we won two hundred dollars by the simple expedient of never picking the favorite, always a middle-runner. It's the law of averages. Everything is average in the long run. The average always wins.

One morning, Nahtasha came down to breakfast and found me reading a newspaper. "Look, it says here that, 'Harvey, the three-thousand-pound, bottle-fed, six-year-old racing buffalo, will take on three quarter horses, one of which will be ridden by Angel Cordero.'" She thought I was pulling her leg. Recently, I'd become something of a joker, a jester. So had Pol. I was teaching him to whistle "The Post-Horn Gallop." "It says here you can pick up free grandstand admission tickets from Price Chopper."

Next day, we were getting ready to go to the racecourse. I wanted to take Pol with us. I thought he would benefit from

23

the experience, maybe add to his repertory. But Nahtasha didn't want him to come. She said he'd get spooked. We've brought him all the way up here, I said. He's been sitting in this room for a week, learning "The Post-Horn Gallop." It hardly seemed fair. So I put him on my arm, and he hauled himself beak over beak onto my shoulder. He let loose a volley of the beginning of "The Post-Horn Gallop": "*Da* da *da* da *da* da da da / DA da DA da DA da DA da ..." He knew what it was all about. It didn't take him long to get into the spirit of things. Nahtasha said she was feeling a bit better. The pain in her chest had eased a bit.

We looked all over for Harvey, but there was no Harvey. Pol was quiet and subdued. Even a little intimidated, I thought. Nahtasha told me to ask about Harvey, so I went to a young woman in a red coat, officiating at the head of the stairs in the grandstand. "Go to the ticket-office window," she told me. "Is that a parrot?" I did as she suggested, but the clerk turned me away as if I was having him on. Same with a Pinkerton "Peace Officer." I went to another Peace Officer, huge and red-faced, with a cracked lower lip. "Ain't none of that," he said. "Not here. Not today. Not ever. No parrots allowed, either." So we went to the Red Spring to drink and have our stomachs almost turned inside out. Pol hopped down and took a brief bath. I began to think I had dreamed the whole thing about Harvey, even though I had been given free grandstand admission tickets from Price Chopper. "Ask her," Nahtasha demanded, as we passed a Coke stand. The girl tittered. "That's a rabbit, isn't it?" she said. "No, really. It's a three-thousand-pound racing buffalo."

But I was having grave doubts. There was certainly no provision on the official race card for such an improbable event. I thought a *moo* might help. Kinda bring Harvey out if he was shy. But it only brought very strange looks. At Pol. I turned my head and glared at him. Pol was watching the pigeons. I tried to convince Nahtasha and myself that a horse in the far distance by the stables looked like a slimmed-down version of a racing buffalo, but she trained her glasses on it and snorted, like a buffalo. "Oh, what the hell," I said. "Let's use these free grandstand tickets anyway. It costs a lot to sit in the stands." So up we climbed, and sat down in two choice seats. Pol began making hiccupping noises and bobbing his head up and down. "Moo!" he said. "Moo!" "I believe you're in our seats." The voice came from behind. Two elderly patrician ladies were about to turf us out of their seats. Pol puffed out his feathers with a loud shuffling noise, like cards. I looked all around. Everyone had elaborate-looking tickets on strings around their necks. "But we got free tickets from Price Chopper," I mumbled. One of the lady attendants came up and told us that grandstand admission meant that we could *stand* in front of the grandstand. Before I could get up, Pol let loose with a test "Moo." I turned to look at him, and, seemingly without opening his beak, he emitted a much louder "MOO." By the time I'd stood up, he'd done a vacuum cleaner, his name five times, the first two bars of "The Post-Horn Gallop," and had started in on little farting noises and something that sounded like "Are You Lonesome Tonight?" As I stood, looking around and wondering where to go, the sound of an Exer-Bike stung my ear. This sound seemed to interest him more than the others, and though I tried to hush him, even tried to grab him, he easily ignored my hushing sounds and just as easily evaded my hand. With a flap of his stumpy wings, he was on my head, his claws digging into my scalp. He went quieter. By a subtle change in his weight, it seemed to me he had his head on one side and was listening for his own sounds, as if they had been coming from somewhere outside himself. Then he blasted the stand with his Exer-Bike.

Nahtasha began to cry, first softly, mostly sniffles, and then a full weep when the vacuum cleaner cut in. "Please, please," said one of the elderly ladies, who had been waiting patiently, perhaps mesmerized, through all this. "Please keep the seats." I heard her steps receding back down the steps. I sat down before she changed her mind. Pol hopped off my head and onto my right shoulder. He had gone quiet again, but as soon as he saw he had my attention, he kick-started his vacuum cleaner and was off to the races again. It roared and swooped, cleaning out any dust and dirt that had anywhere managed to conceal itself. It was pulling in the world, sucking it all up, sucking us all in, to a kind of mindless repeating memory, nothing lost. I started to laugh, and was surprised after a while to hear my laugh coming from the machine. Nahtasha had stopped crying. She was smiling. Everyone was staring at the bird, whose head was bouncing up and down. Suddenly, the sound of hoofbeats came from inside his closed beak, and a muffled moo. Out of the corner of my eye I thought I saw a buffalo race onto the track, a besatinned and besilked jockey clinging to his hump, a jockey bright as a jester, lacking only bells. The sound of bells came from my shoulder, an inch from my right ear.

The Kiss

He was still wobbling when he got into his car and began the drive home. He noticed all the dead birds on the road: a wing rising from the pavement here, a tail there. His mood wasn't helped by being pinned against the inside of his back door and having his face beslobbered, all the while a wild yodeling noise going off within inches of his ear. He fought off the dog's welcome and after a while the animal subsided. When he himself had calmed down, he toasted three English muffins. It was a foolish thing to have done, that whale-watch trip. Suppose the boat had gone down (once or twice he wished it had). What would have happened to the dog he'd locked on the house on a diet of Kibbles and Chunks, with water? (True, he'd poured in more K and C than usual, and filled the drinking bowl to the very brim, just in case. The dog would have lasted at least two days. Enough time for the police to locate his address from the driver's license he kept in a waterproof case.) He poured himself a sugar-free root beer to go with the three English muffins. To steady himself, he skimmed the sports page of the Times. He lay down, and stayed prone for an hour, the dog under the bed beating time with his tail against the floor. Better not waste the rest of the day. He took the dog by the collar and, bent over in a Groucho Marx crouch, hung on while the dog ran out onto the unkempt lawn to get affixed to his rope. Then he went into the garage he'd turned into a studio. Nothing. No finbacks, right, or sperm. Not even a dolphin. Only nausea.

He read what he had written the night before.

He couldn't do it. Instead of getting the right tone for a

popular, money-making novel, he ended up writing like an idiot. He just didn't know how ordinary people talked. Straight from college into the office. He tore it up. It was a foolish risk and decision. He couldn't write. He could have retained his passion for literature and left the writing of it to others. He lay back again and closed his eyes.

Hairs covered his black canvas shoes. Hairs covered his socks. What a shaggy dog. He slipped on socks, then he slipped on shoes. He no longer bothered to flap them about to dislodge some of the pelt. The shaggy dog bounded about whining, bouncing off the walls, delighted at the new day, the new life. Every day the same. Now and then he'd give a wild yelp, as if someone had just stomped on his tail. "Yes, yes. Hang on. It's not even dawn yet." He shivered. He wasn't even awake. It had become habit. The dog didn't need to bound on the bed and holler in his ear at the first bird's song. The temperature had dropped the night before and he was wakened in the middle of it by the acrid smell of burning. He realized it was the gas heater under the floor, just outside the bedroom. So he'd pulled on a hairy blanket and gone back to sleep.

The dog was now yelping like a boarhound, sounding off something awful, out of his mind with excitement. Immediate gratification. Now. Live in the *Now*. The same every morning. "I told you, hang on." Something hurt his foot in the shoe. He pulled off the right sock and shoe and sleepwalked out of the bedroom toward the bathroom. A yell seemed to come from inside his head, blowing the top off. Next thing he knew he was hopping about on one leg. A smell of burning came from below. He'd walked barefoot onto the hot grill over the heater. The dog burst out in sympathetic howling. "Ay, ay!" "Yo-o-o-o-w-l!" Pain-crazed, he lunged for the dog, grabbing him by the collar, and hung on while the dog himself seemed to burst through doors, slam back bolts, turn locks, and launch them both onto the lawn, where he attached himself to the rope and lay down in the dawn's early light, birds singing, the sky clear as if scoured by a Brillo pad. Vast emptiness. The pain in the foot came back. The dog was opening and shutting his jaws. "OK. OK." He hobbled back into the house. Put a few dog biscuits into one of the bowl's cups, and ran water into the other. He hobbled back out. "There. Biscuits in a bowl. Water in a bowl. How do you like these common miracles?" The dog nearly knocked him flat. Back in the house he grabbed ice from the freezer and held it to his foot. After the initial shock, it began to work. The burn became a numb ache. Then he went and opened the heater's grill, slamming back the lever to OFF. He never remembered turning it ON. He looked out of the window. There was Josh humping another dog, but not from the right end. And not the right sex. He had a German shepherd's head clamped between his elbows and was working away with mighty thrusts. The shepherd was snarling. He twisted round, and, grabbing the smaller dog from the right end, gave much better than he got. The snarling rose in pitch. "Oh, Jesus!" A whirling, teeth-baring, frantic fight had begun with, as usual, Josh getting much the worse of the encounter. "*Jesus!*" He rushed out again, barefoot, not even remembering to pull on sweat pants over pajama bottoms. Screaming, he hurled himself at the battle, which broke up in a flash, one dog bounding off like a deer, the other leaping up to lick his master's face. And still the birds sang, and still the sky was clear, turning from pale to darker blue. A baby robin on his first flight was churbling away, pestering its mother for worms. Caterpillars were dangling on threads, or floating about on them. Birds were giving chase. It was too much, the racket. It seemed Nature was bursting its bounds. Eat and be eaten. Me, me, me. He staggered back to bed.

*

It had been like this for the past three months, since his wife had decided it was best for both of them if he moved out, and took the damn dog with him too. He'd been about to make the same suggestion, with the differences that he was going to suggest that she move out and take the dog. But the idea was good, whatever the details. He let his head drop to the pillow. *Every day I did not spend in solitude was wasted.* He sneezed, again and again. It was the pollen season. As he'd watched the previous evening, standing in the east, framed by the garage door, he'd seen billions of pollen grains streaming past the setting sun like meteor showers. He sneezed again. And shivered. He pulled the blanket up. Immediately a shower of dog hairs flew into his face. He coughed. The blanket was covered with hairs. The dog had been sleeping on him all night. No wonder he'd had nightmares of suffocation, great hairy women sitting on his face, women with tails.... He recalled the morning he'd woken, just after the separation. He'd turned in the bed, as he'd done hundreds of times, to kiss his wife while she slept. But instead of meeting soft, gentle, sweet-smelling skin and moist full lips, his lips had met something feral and foul-smelling, something cold and wet, something—he shuddered at the memory—that leaped on him and licked him with such fury he didn't know where he was. He'd had to beat it off. Since then, he'd tried closing the bedroom door at night, but the dog easily pushed it open. He'd tried locking it, but the lock was broken, and he'd lost the key early on. (In fact, only a few days after he arrived, he had to climb out of the window. One of his neighbors, whom he hadn't yet met, looked up from the various machines he was tinkering with in his sandy yard. He called the police, who happened to be his son, whose high school reunion was being held nearby. So, when the law came running out, gun in hand, there was no place to turn except back to the window. Which was now blocked with the leaping form of a black hound, off the leash, and not happy at the turn of events, and who took off for the open road. The whole neighborhood was now roused: Mr. Pulver, the lawnmower repairer, Mr. Lange the gas-station owner, and the lady next door who worked for local taxes, part-time. All the details are not worth recounting, except to note that it took the whole morning to retrieve the dog from miles away, and that the lady next door was finally persuaded not to press public morals charges, since the front of his pajamas kept flapping open. And so, from that moment, he and the dog were locked in together, as it were. In short time, he had acquired a reputation for eccentricity. It suited him fine.)

*

And now he had become father, mother, wife, husband, friend, everything, to the animal, who would never let him out of his sight. If, for a short moment, he passed into the dog's oblivion, Josh would set up such a racket that he sounded like a convocation of banshees. The neighbors had already gone to Town Hall and denounced them both as a public nuisance. When that hadn't produced much, they'd hinted at various fates for dog and master if something wasn't done. So, when he could, he'd take Josh everywhere with him. Eventually, the dog was reassured enough to be able to tolerate up to three hours of his absence. But it almost wasn't worth it, since the greeting Josh gave him when he reappeared was so wild it became close to a terror for him, leaping up head-high like a circus dog, making no noises dogs ever made, scratching at him with his claws as if trying to get a foothold and climb him, great wet tongue-lashings with a tongue the size of a baleen whale's. And always that foul dog breath enveloping him in a fetid smoke of decay and mortality. Sometimes the dog got so excited that, even when he was put outside on his rope, he'd tear round and round the tree he was tied to until he'd lashed himself to it as securely as Odysseus was lashed to his mast. There he'd stand, baffled, panting, legs attempting to run still, wound round in restriction he couldn't understand. Once or twice his owner had been sorely tempted to give him a few fast kicks to the ribs while he had him at his mercy. Getting the animal unwound was another story. It's enough to say that the best method was found to be to grab the dog in its helpless condition and run with him hugged to the chest round and round the ancient pole, spinning out wider and wider, like those Mexican Indians in their sacred ceremony which consists of hurling themselves from the top of a high pole, their ankle attached to the top platform by a rope which pays out as they fall lower and lower, circle wider and wider, until they almost scrape the dust of the plaza with their noses.

*

He was sitting at the old rented typewriter. Nothing coming. Nothing going. There was a beating of wings, like inspiration. Then a scrabbling noise, and he realized it wasn't inside his head. It was like the chipmunks over his head when he took naps in the small house. Chipmunks running to hurl themselves head-first down the drainpipe, shooting out the other end near the birch tree. Sometimes he left Kibbles and Bits for them, arranged neatly in a circle. The noise got louder, above his head, so he looked up from his reverie. It demanded attention. There was a fat adolescent robin battling valiantly against the small window high up above the garage doors. It kept falling back onto the shelf below, gathering its breath, then launching itself against the glass again. "Go out the same way you came in," he called to it. "This is the way I came in," said the bird, now hopping onto a rafter and looking about jerkily, but with seeming disinterest, as if to say: No sweat. I can get out of here any time I want. What I can see through I can fly through. Crash. By now the dog had noticed the commotion and came in through the side door, stretching the rope to its limit, staring upward, chops agape. A ladder was needed. "Out!" he called to the dog, who was wagging his tail furiously, ears up. "Out, I said!" More wagging, and this time accompanied by a note that could have come from a horn in the Black Forest. "For Chrissake!" He dragged Josh out and looped the rope round and round a sapling to shorten it. "Stay!" The metal ladder was long enough. He reached out his arm and the bird went into a frenzy of fluttering against the glass, screeching. The dog was now bellowing. Out of the corner of his eye, he could see the sapling thrashing about as if in a nuclear firestorm. The bird had a good strong bill, with which he attacked the rescuing hand. "Ow! Little devil!" He backed down the ladder slowly, trying to do a breathing exercise to block out the pain from the jabs and the noise. Finally, he reached the door and opened his hand. The bird took off in a straight low line across the lawn, as if it knew where it was going, straight toward the road. An adult robin took off after it. He thought he saw a car swerve. He wanted to go out to check if what he feared had happened had happened. In the sky, grackles and robins were mobbing a buzzard. It seemed all the birds in the world were raising their voices at something or other. He undid the dog, who leaped up and beslobbered him with an endless tongue. He went back into the garage, where he was used to spending most of the days. Opposite the side door it had a small window that overlooked the Pulvers' back yard. He'd spent quite a bit of time glancing through this window, hoping for a glimpse of the daughter. No luck.

*

Something caught his eye, which had glazed over staring at the sheet in the typewriter. He snuck over to get a better view. Mrs. Pulver, in wrap-around beige skirt and boomy blouse, was staring deep into an old-fashioned washing-machine. From under the attached wringer, she picked out of the enamel tub flat socks, flat shirts, flat underwear, so many stiff pelts. She was looking at them with some sort of puzzlement. Mr. Pulver arrived, and stared into the tub too. He was down to undershirt and cut-off jeans. All around them the yard was littered with machine parts of lawnmowers. He stepped back, and banged into the covered barbecue. It shook on its stand. His wife picked her nose, not noticing. And then, out of the back door came their daughter, eighteen, in black swimwear, cut high at the thighs.

Since he first saw her, it had puzzled him how two such parents could have produced such a daughter. Clearly, she had just gotten up. Her hair was like Medusa's, but her figure was a wonder. She stuck a finger in her bathing suit and ran it round the leg. It was too tight. He watched as she went back into the house and returned with a bunch of black grapes. She popped them like pills, mouth opening wide. She went back inside. And returned in a blue and white bathing suit. Did she know he was watching? She had more breakfast in her other hand. A red liquid, red as the liquid apothecaries used to have in their vast jars, which he remembered from childhood. Among the lawnmowers, there was a boat with an outboard motor. And a bicycle. He noticed that her father and mother had given up on the washing machine. Mr. Pulver had picked up a hose and started to water a small vegetable patch. Slyly, he sprinkled his daughter, who screamed. There was a double-barrelled ghetto blaster on the white metal picnic table. She moved toward it, and as she did—did she look up and see him in the window? The girl had begun to obsess him. He thought of phoning her, inviting her out. Or phone and say nothing, just to hear her voice say hello.

*

He hadn't been prepared for her arrival. He'd had a phone call now and then, mostly consisting of recitations of his failings and weakness, his dependency, his hidden dark side, his hatred of women and commitment, his lack of energy, his middle-age crisis, and so on. With most of which he agreed. She hadn't come alone. She had two friends in tow, with their two sons, about five and eight. He hadn't seen her in the three months since he'd left. Why had she arrived, with no advance notice? She looked and felt like a stranger. He assumed it had something to do with gathering material for her divorce file. Just what, he hadn't a clue.

"Here, boys! Come and meet the dog!" It was the mother of the two boys. Presumably another junior high teacher. The man was presumably her husband, and presumably—presumably nothing. There were no introductions, and no explanations. He figured they'd be gone by the end of the two-day weekend. He felt sure they'd be gone by then. If not sooner. They'd have to entertain themselves. He had little money. He knew exactly how long it would be until his savings were exhausted, how long it would take him to renovate the soil and plant a garden, how long until he knew if he was a writer or not. So he knew pretty well how long it would be before he shot himself. He would sometimes help himself get to sleep by working out the details—how he would bury himself in one of the dunes, for example. He still hadn't figured a way of how to prevent the dog from digging him up. "What's his name?" "Excuse me?" "The dog. What's his name?" "Oh. Josh." "Josh? That's a funny name for a dog, isn't it, boys? What's it short for? Joshua?" "Joshu." Before she could query that, the dog, who was already excited

35

at meeting strangers, began to get out of hand, squirming about and whining.

"Why don't you take him for a walk?" It was a wicked thing to suggest. Where did he get such ideas? His wife intervened. "I don't think that's such a good idea. You know how crazy that dog is—" The dog shot her a crazed look. He knew a couple of words in the English language, and one of them was "walk." He began bouncing about on his hind legs for fully a minute, letting off the usual yodels and bugles like a male wapiti in rut. "Oh, what a cute dog!" exclaimed the mother. "Can I pet him?" "Not if you value your arm," he said. "No. Only kidding. He loves people. He's like me that way. Loves being petted. Loves to be taken for a WALK."

The dog went crazier at the magic *walk,* and practically flew on his hind legs across the lawn, stretching his rope till it vibrated and constricted his windpipe to a thin tube through which volumes of gulped air screamed and clattered. "He's choking himself," the older boy observed scientifically, scarcely looking up from his Godzilla comic-book. He'd hardly raised his eyes from its pages since he arrived. "Do you want to WALK?" "Don't do that!" his wife called out. "You know—"

"Oh, please!" begged the five-year old. "Just a short walk. *Please!*" "Well, all right," came his mother's dubious reply. "If it's all right with your father. What do you think, darling?" She turned, but her husband had vanished. "He does this," she explained with exasperation in her voice. "Men. Just when you need them—" "Who needs them?" said his wife. And they didn't see the husband again until that evening when, with a grunt and no explanation, he came in and went to bed. "All right, then," the woman muttered. "Sure. You can take him for a walk." "You might never see them again," he murmured. "What? What do you mean?" "Only a joke," he answered. "It's his sense of humor," his wife added. "He thinks it's funny.

Him and that damned dog. Do you know it ate my wedding gown?" "Ate it?" "Every last scrap." "He was only a pup." Commiserations were cut short as it took three adults and two children to subdue the dog enough to substitute rope for leash, and reduce him to a state of comparative calm. Then came instructions on how to walk the dog. "OK, now. Whatever you do, and whatever he does, don't let go. He got off the rope a few mornings back," he explained to the mother, "just as I was taking him back into the house, and I had to run in my pajamas and bare feet practically all the way to town. And that's three miles." "We won't! We won't!" Even the comic-book devourer had entered into the spirit of things, and didn't notice the wind take Godzilla and whip him into a ragged hedge of old lilac bushes back of the house. To the kids it must have felt like harnessing the wind. Because hardly had they grabbed hold before they were both pulled off their feet with a huge jerk. The older boy had lashed the leash once round his wrist so there was no extricating as he managed to scramble up. His brother got up too, but had lost his grip. "Let me take him for a walk too! It's my turn! Maaa, he won't let me take the dog for—" His elder brother, grim-faced, was beating him off with one arm, and with the other trying to grab anything to stay his headlong rush—sapling, tree, mailbox, anything. He preserved a determined silence. His mother charged after them, screaming. She could see Josh heading straight for the busy road along which teenagers, in souped-up hot-rods, were heading for the beach, radios blaring. "Come back! Come back!" she screamed. "I've got him! I've got him!" the older boy called back, just before he fell on his face in a pile of old branches and brush which had been left out for the town woodchipping truck to work on. The five-year-old was far behind, and his mother not far behind him. When they arrived, panting, they were in time to see Josh with his right rear leg raised over the unfortunate eight-year-old who appeared to be in a daze, as if he'd survived a cyclone. His mother was hysterical. But before she had time to retrieve one offspring and protect the other, Josh, tail wagging furiously, had begun a humping movement. With one rush, he tore the leash out of the eight-year-old's hand and was on top of his brother, pumping like a maniac, his pink plunger tight up against the child's body. The dog was taller than the child. They were almost face to chest. "Look!" cried the child, "she really likes me! Look, how she's hugging me!" "Get down, you disgusting beast!" screamed the mother, frantically waving her arms above her head, too afraid to do anything else. "Get down! Go get his master!" But nobody was in a position to do anything, except her, and she was hysterical. Luckily, the dog's master soon made his appearance. "Get off him, you stupid animal," he said, and grabbed the dog by the collar, hauling him off. "I told you he was a bit of handful. He's rather unredeemed, I'm afraid." "She likes me! She really likes me!" "That dog's a menace. It should be locked up. I'm calling the police." "She really likes me! Can I have a dog just like Josh? Can I, mummy, please?" "And look what he's done to my son. Just look at the state that boy's in." "There's plenty of water. A new well was dug a month ago." "If this is your idea of a joke—" "I had no idea the dog was so strong—" "Liar! Lisa has told me all about you."

*

After the storm was a calm, of sorts. At least, after long showers all round, the mother took her brood to the beach. His wife had a headache and wanted to lie down. "I'll use your room," she said. "The other one's already occupied. At least you've got sheets on your bed, even if they haven't been changed in three months." "Two," he corrected. He went outside and sat down on the lawn. He pulled Josh over to look for ticks. He had found two and was in the process of getting his nails under them before he realized his wife standing over him. "Come with me," she commanded. "Can't leave the dog," he replied. "He'll holler up a storm." "I've got something I want to show you. I'd like an explanation." He heaved himself to his feet. "Look," he said to the dog. "Just give me five, OK?" He began to walk away, but something made him look back. He was presented with the tableau of the dog, at the end of his tether, on hind legs, heraldically throttling himself. The more impossible he found it to breathe, the tighter he pulled the rope. There was theatrical silence. Then a cough, and a drawn-out howl like the all-clear. "My God!" He ran and pushed the dog over. It lay panting, and then stretched out, still. He went inside. She was standing by the mirror in the bedroom. "What's this? It's still wet." He looked hard at where she was pointing. What he saw startled him a bit. His own face. He had never been one to look at himself in the mirror. For one thing, he'd been warned against vanity as a child. For another, he had nothing to be vain about. What he saw was a man who seemed to be growing a beard, but without intention. As if his face had just decided for itself. And then he got caught up in the idea of the eyes in the mirror staring at the eyes outside, and so on, back and forth, into the infinity of the self, staring into into into ... *is to study the self. To study the self is to forget the self. To forget the self is to be enlightened by all things.* There was nothing to stare into. It was all there; all stared out and consumed in the looking. Vast emptiness. Nothing to discover. No secret ... "Who put it there?"

He turned, then looked back to where she was pointing. A purple kiss was on the mirror. It just was. He gave a big laugh. And then another. He found it difficult to stop laughing. Eventually, he said: "It's a kiss. That's all. A kiss!" "Who put it there?" "I'm really sorry," he said, "but I have no idea how it got

39

there. It must have been there all along. I just never noticed."
"It's a cheap brand. No mature woman wears that color. And it's
still damp." He touched it lightly with his right forefinger, which
he then held up. "What are you pointing at?" "Pointing? Oh
no! There's nothing." "So who is she?" "She? Nobody. There's
nobody." He could see his wife was totally unconvinced. But
why would she even be concerned? Something like compassion
swept over him and he moved toward her. "Don't touch me!"
she said. "Who is she?" What could he say? He thought for a
while. "Well, it could be this. Ever since I moved in here I've
been receiving anonymous phone calls. Just yesterday I got ten
in a row, at three-minute intervals. I'd pick up, and there'd be a
click. It got so bad I phoned the phone company and they told
me to pick up the phone and say: 'All right, operator. You can
start tracing this call now.' Of course, they can't. But by dialing
4 just after I say 'All right' et cetera, that activates a series of
clicks, and the person at the other end thinks something official
is happening. If you look on the table you'll see lists of times.
The phone company asked me to keep a list of times." "What's
all this have to do with the kiss on the mirror?" "There are lots
of young girls around. You know what gets into their heads.
I say hello to them and they never reply. I hear them giggling
behind my back." "So?" "Well, there's a girl next door. I often
see her staring at me. And a few nights ago the phone continued
to ring after I put the lights out. Someone could see I was still
in, and that my car was still there. Once I didn't answer for
half an hour, and it still rang. Someone must have been able to
see the house." "Look. You can tell me. I hate deceit." "I live
alone. I see nobody. I don't know anybody. All this is starting
to seem very silly to me." "Not that I care, you understand. You
can do what you want. I just want to know." "Please." "Maybe
she crept in while you were out and put the kiss there. Or
while you were asleep." "This may sound strange to you, but

I think that kiss was there from the very start. Before I moved in, even. Maybe that is why I've felt so good here." There was a long pause. "Don't you get lonely? Aren't you afraid?" There was another long pause, during which an adolescent robin's insistent screeching for worms could be heard. There he was, just outside the bedroom window, stubby, fat, no tail to speak of. Full of a crazy kind of life.

TULE FOG

is snaking back along sluices and streams. During the day, it had climbed like a vast cloud of midgies to the top of houses. Now, at evening, it is descending, falling back into the waterways, settling on the reeds. Many crops round here are produced with no watering. Nasturtiums spread their spicy leaves over rockeries. Geraniums add a tincture of crimson to windowboxes. The fog blends and dims. The world empties. Blankness fills it. Heat, damp heat, fills the blankness.

In the attic, the wood has a dog-bitten appearance. He is wondering how anyone can explain that. From somewhere below, he hears a man's muffled jeer. He knows the man is standing on the bridge, fog cutting him off from his image. Heat bumps against the angle of the roof, and is trapped. Silence in the empty house.

He kneels on the boards, places his mouth against the wood. Lukewarm. The wood is lukewarm. Words form on his lips; are prevented by the press of rough wood. He stands up and finds it hard to breathe. He looks out of the dormer window.

He looks out the window. All the light is gone. Not even the drifting fog is visible. He runs his fingers along the smooth maple window ledge. He remembers the pencil box his uncle had carved for him when he was a child. The lid slid smoothly in grooves. A little gouged indent gave the finger purchase on the lid. He remembers opening and closing. He could never bring himself to put anything inside.

*

She has put on *Oxygène*. The synthesized music cools the house. He dumps a frozen cup of Hawaiian punch into what's left of the iced tea. Ninety-eight and rising. Here, a record for July. He has still not wiped up all the stains of mercurochrome from a bottle he dropped the week before. It makes the bathroom look like the scene of an axe-murder, she says. He lifts the glass. Condensation beads and drips. He goes into his study. He picks up a piece of paper that accompanies the Realistic Low Noise cassette tape: "This tape reprograms the unconscious to automatically change the way you eat and drink and *how you see yourself*. You may fall asleep while listening to it. It makes no difference. The tape will have its effect, anyway. You must listen to it each day. It takes about a month to achieve full re-programming...." He is about to put it on when his wife comes in, carrying the newspaper. She startles him so much that he makes a violent hiccup and sits stark upright in this chair. To cover, he asks: "Want to do something?" She tosses the paper onto a gathering pile in the corner. "There's nothing more stimulating than my boredom right now." "Do you want to see *Pink Frankenstein*?" He'd showered for the nth time an hour before. His hair still stuck flat to his skull and felt like a mud helmet. She collapsed onto the floor and went into a half-lotus. She said: "I heard about this big black man who got on the bus. He was clutching his stomach, and blood was seeping through his jacket. He refused all help until a cop made him open his coat, and a white hand dripping with diamonds fell to the floor." "Do you want to go out tonight? How about a fish dinner?" "I've got a planter's wart on the bottom of my big toe. When we were sunbathing on the pier earlier this morning I found it. I thought it was a stone at first. But it's not. It's a planter's wart." "Like a planter's peanut?" He hid the cassette under some typewriter sheets, and then tried to hide the typewriter sheets. She pulled herself to her feet and slouched into the bathroom. He followed. She said: "I wish I could write. I see so many awful things. Did I tell you what I saw yesterday as I was coming home from buying those black shoes that gave me the blister, after work?" "We could eat pizza, if you wanted." She is squeezing a whitehead. The mirror needs dusting. He stares. "Must you keep slurping that tea?" she says. "It's by choice." She finishes. He looks away. They leave the bathroom, Indian-file, she ahead.

"I saw a crowd of people. And then something made me look up into one of the trees on the corner, you know, by Bono's. There were broken branches all over the place, and a pair of brown corduroy slacks was stuck high in the tree. Everyone was crowding round the body of a young black woman who'd thrown herself off a tenth-floor balcony. At least they said she was young. You couldn't tell." "I'll clean up the mess in the bathroom later. I hate when you hint." She has taken her Gillette Body Haircurler from a drawer in the bedroom and brought it into the bathroom. She plugs it in by the sink. He has followed. "With all those spikes it looks like a masochist's dildo," he said. "Look, why don't you go listen to your hypnotist record?" He didn't know she knew. "My back must be tanned real good. It hurts something awful," he said. "OK. OK. So you can come with me. You're pathetic. I'm going to get some nectarines, and *David Bowie's Greatest Hits* and *The Thin Man* from the library." "No. I'm in a good mood now. I don't want to spoil it by going out." "You think it's bad now? I'm getting my period soon." She stuck the curler into her hair, and made twisting motions. "Do you want to have sex?" he asked. "Cover our bodies with vaseline and roll about on the bed?" "Get me John Travolta. And air conditioning. Here, sharpen this eyeshadow." "Lucky you're an old lady." She went into the bedroom and dared the full-length mirror. "There. Do I look rapeable now?" "If you'll stay still long enough. You're always on the move. Are you sure those shorts aren't too provocative?" "Well, if I had big tits and nice legs … But with little knockers and knock-knees, I'll be OK." "I adore you." She sat down on the bed. She peeled an old band-aid from her blistered toe and stuck on a new one. Then she pulled on her new black shoes. "I heard a woman on TV the other night. She said, 'I like to look beautiful because I represent God.' Sure you don't want to come with me?" "I'd come, but I'd have to get dressed first. I'll long for your return," he replied. "I was going to call you yesterday from a pay phone, and tell you how much I loved you. But I lost my dime."

After she left, the dog whined, and kept on whining. He took him for a walk. Toby leaped up at the leash, grabbing it in his mouth, taking himself for a walk. Simon was dragged along behind. Sometimes the line would go slack, but then it would snap taut as if a Hemingway 500-pound marlin was on the other end, and Toby would leap forward to bury himself nose-deep in something delicious and invisible. Simon tried to anticipate where Toby would rush to splash his presence in controlled doses, hoping to be able to prepare himself for one of those socket-severing jolts. But, from walk to walk, Toby seldom favored the same place twice. Several times Simon had almost lost an arm when Toby, following a scent to a telegraph pole or whatever, would first go one way, to one side, and then instantly reverse field to the other side, and back again, three or four times. This was not indecision, even less was it malign. It was just that he had to follow the vagaries of his nose, which is to say, the route of his interest. That was how he thought: instantly, unerringly. But always after the fact, always as the resurrector of histories that would be lost forever had he not happened by. And then he forgot them instantly. He kept none of them, going onto the next and retaining nothing. Simon envied Toby's world, or his own version of it: rich in ancient places in the brain, self-correcting instantly. Kind of empty, yet constantly creative. Only the rains of yesterday stood between him and some ultimate immediate unmediated knowledge. Or so he thought, in a kind of contradiction.

They walked by, ages ten or eleven. "Dingo," he heard repeated. So he turned. "No, he's not a dingo. Have you ever seen a dingo?" "Sure," said the shorter one, in shorts, from the beach. "They're bigger," he said. "How big?" asked the taller one, in bathing suit. He held his hand a foot above Toby. "So big. About so big." The shorter one had begun walking away, but the taller girl came toward him. "How do you know Bingo?" she asked. "Bingo? Bingo? Oh, well I don't. I—" She eyed him suspiciously. She had been warned about such as him. "You see," he said, "I thought you said 'dingo'. And that's an Australian wild—" But she'd already moved to join her companion. When he looked back, slowly as Toby was wetting down a small and soon to be stunted yucca, he saw them both turn and take him in well, as if memorizing his appearance. And he memorized theirs. This must go into the story. Funny how anything suddenly seems important when you're working on something. He was brought out of his reverie by Toby whining longingly at another dog across the street. He got into fights out of pure exuberance and desire for friendship. He didn't seem to know the rules. Smothering another dog with affection was no guarantee of affection returned. There are rites and rituals, formalities and protocol. Toby was oblivious to them all. Owners of female dogs would lash out at him with their feet, but there was no telling them that Toby was a virgin dog and meant no harm.

*

It was already well on into the afternoon. He wandered to the front door again to see if the mail had arrived. There was one letter. "Dear Mr. Crown: Have you ever considered that one day you could be sued for $1,000,000? It's not as unlikely as you may think. In today's society, lawsuits are common. You could lose almost everything. That's why we want to introduce you to the INA GUARDIAN Program." He stuffed it into his pocket. Back in the kitchen, he opened the fridge. Remains of softshell crabs. A quiver of repulsion ran down his spine. Had he eaten any of the eyes? Humidity and heat formed a small cloud that drifted back into the refrigerator. His mother-in-law's voice seemed to come from the back of the motor. He responded without having heard the full question. He forgot she was still there. When had she arrived? Yesterday? The day before? A week ago? He said: "Some experts say the portrait's authentic. Others don't agree. That's all I know." This time the voice seemed to come from the freezer. "Oh my. Does that mean he may have painted the wrong person?" There was a crash, and then a childish wail. Then his wife's voice. "I told you not to climb up there. I told you you'd fall." Another wail. "But you didn't tell me *when*. It's all your f-a-a-ult!" Her sister's kid. There for another hour, or eternity, whichever came first. The child was deposited in some dark place deep in the house to recover. His mother-in-law stepped into the kitchen. "Of course you do! Sonntag. Frederick Sonntag, precursor of the Ashcan School. Known as an American Impressionist—" "What's he do? Birdcalls?" She stomped her foot. The noise startled him. He'd only meant to show interest. Actually, he'd meant to irritate. "And why are you limping? He didn't know he was. "In shiatsu they'd know what to do," she said. "For what?" "Your limp." "It was bending all day yesterday. In the garden. Back of the legs." "Oh, *that!* It's the hamstring," she informed him. "Yes, I remember I used to have one as a kid. Had a little wheel he'd get in and run around." "I give up! An impossible person! Won't you ever get serious? Won't you ever grow up?" Won't you ever get a job? "Are you kidding?

The world's adolescent. Look at the headlines in the newspaper you're about to read. 'Heart Victim's Body Bursts Into Flames.' And that's a respected daily journal." "I am not about to read it. I found it in the cellar. Your dog's done his business in my room." Snooping around. "What did you say?" "I thought I heard a *sound.* The mail! I thought I heard the mail." He dashed off to the letterbox, realizing halfway there that he'd already pocketed the mail. But he went through with it anyhow. To his surprise, a small pile, of different colors, sat under the cloacal slit. Probably shoved through by his neighbor, a salesman of some sort or other, whose name resembled his: Krone. He hadn't delivered the misdirected mail out of civic responsibility or good neighborliness, however. He did it so he could get a closer look at what he disapproved of. Since he disapproved of just about everything, he seldom went without his reward. Two or three pieces of junk mail. If the senders know it's junk mail, and have a pretty good idea concerning its fate, why do they continue to send it? Pure habit, he thought. Or some sort of tax break. Every useless cause has a tax break behind it. The more they send the less they pay. There was also a letter, buried in the pile, from his mother. He took out his Swiss Army knife, and pulled open a blade, the one used to pry Boy Scouts out of horses' hooves. He jabbed it into the envelope and ripped it open. As usual. The same kind of stuff he'd received from his mother since he left home:

"My Dears:

What was wrong with your phone yesterday. I rang you eight o'clock last evening, a lady answered and I kept asking if it was you Bertha several times but she never answered me so I hung up—" And so on. Read: "Your wife answered the phone. But when the bitch recognized your mother's voice she refused to reply." That was the accusation. He didn't bother to read the rest. He heard his mother-in-law's voice, like a car burning rubber. And he recalled he'd promised to buy some Earl Grey tea on his way home from the library yesterday, but had forgotten. It was for her latest literary soiree, and her latest literary acquisition, Georges. He'd been a famous surrealist in his time, but quit, he said, because his nighttime automatic writing turned out to be everything he'd read the previous day. Now he was a successful editor back east. Maybe Georges would look at his work. But not after he'd forgotten to get his favorite Earl Grey. Actually, he'd gotten sidetracked passing the Oasis Motel. There was a young girl on vacation with her family. She was doing laps in the pool, then climbing out and lying on the chaise-lounge, face down, hips rocking, reaching up behind to untie her halter, throwing her hair over the chaise end, stopping her hips, pumping her legs up and down as if in time to some interior headset, pulling her long hair up so her nape could get some sun, or maybe drying the roots of her hair. He had walked closer, as if to inspect the quality of the pool. As he did so, she reached under the chaise and pulled out a book: *Airport.* Suddenly she possessed all the pizzazz of a wet towel. But he couldn't stop himself from watching as she reached into her parents' bag and pulled out a bunch of grapes. She ate them, one after the other, without even tasting them, he was sure. Like a tortoise: one slow bite and one slow swallow. One sentence was enough to break the spell forever. "Can you imagine them," she asked her mother, "bringing their tupperware all the way from Germany. You can't get it in the stores."

Yes, Georges it was. They were sitting in the front room sipping Darjeeling, by the scent of it. Simon's mother-in-law gave him an accusing glance. Georges didn't seem to mind. "And, my darling," he intoned, "I had just brought Thomas a perambulator! Can you believe it? That's the fate of aging homosexuals. They buy perambulators for the babies of all their normal friends. Hundreds in a lifetime—" "How are you Georges? I'm sorry about the tea. I forgot." "Don't mention it, old boy. I was just telling Matilda here about the last time I saw Penna—Sandro—Penna, the poet. Know him?" "Afraid not." "Well, it matters not." "Do tell it again. Simon will enjoy it. He has a good sense of humor if he applies himself. He could be a writer." He was about to pour himself a cup of tea, but realized it was piping hot. She's kept it under a tea cozy. The air itself was like a tea-cozy. He began to sweat again. "Well, it seems that the little *gamins* of Trastevere got poor Sandro into all sorts of shady deals. Blackmarket deals, you understand. One day, one of these little devils persuaded Sandro to buy up a huge stock of U.S. strawberry jam in cans. And he stored them in his bedroom, which was the door next to the one we were in; he only had two rooms, if you discount the bathroom. Well, we were talking about this and that on one of those hot Roman afternoons not unlike this one, when there was a huge explosion. My dears, an *immense* explosion! The house rocked to its foundations, I'm sure. The neighbors must have thought it was another air-raid attack. Anyhow, we rushed into the bedroom, and everything was coated with strawberry jam; it dripped from the walls, hung in great red globs from the light fixtures, and stuck to the windows so you couldn't see out!" Simon smiled. "Sometimes I feel this house is dripping strawberry jam," he said. There was a yelping from outside. "If you'll excuse me, I'd better go see what ails him."

Toby was pulling at his rope. The lilac bush to which he was attached was about to be uprooted. Simon called to him, "Good dog," but that didn't have any effect. There was an old dog he hadn't seen before on the lawn next door, doing what old dogs do. It must have been this that infuriated Toby, not getting a rise out of him. Just then, the salesman-neighbor came out of the house and called the old dog in, first fixing Simon and

Toby with a laser look. Time to come in, Simon told Toby, and slipped the leash. The dog broke Simon's grip on his collar and dashed onto the neighbor's lawn. Smelling furiously where the old dog had lain, he lifted his leg a dozen times and saturated the whole area, fast, and then trotted back, and into the house. *He's forgotten everything. The moment it's done.* Simon hadn't noticed when his wife returned. But there she was, catching the corner of his eye. She was trying to wave off a yellow butterfly that was hovering above her navel as she lay sunbathing. There was hardly any sun left. He loomed over her, a vast shadow. "I'm only doing this, you understand, to get my extra dose of Vitamin D." Yes, this was the way he'd finish the story. It would be all the high points of everything he'd remembered, and could use; five years in one day, concentrated into something like ultimate immediate knowledge. And he would continue— how? (Where would he fit in the fact that she'd brushed her teeth from side to side, as if she were polishing shoes? Later, later. There's time. There's no time.) But then. Dare he tell the truth? He'd woven in some. What was it, if what he wrote was the way he wished things had been? Ironies were signs of multiplicity, so: an ironic relationship based on what, love (his "wife")? An ironic relationship based on a certain—he couldn't bring himself to say what ("himself"). And a relationship based on certain valencies ("Toby"). He thought: There are worse myths to live by. He doubted it would work. And if it did, would it make him feel better? He gathered up some typed sheets as he passed the study, and climbed up to the attic. He looked out the dormer window of the empty, silent house. He couldn't afford it any more. He'd leave soon. Tule fog was beginning to form along sluices and streams. He slid the top of the pencil box open, and then closed. He did this three or four times. A dog barked in the far distance.

Lem

Lem Sees a Ghost

She spent months looking for the right perfume. I went often too. Altman's, Bloomingdales, Lord and Taylor … We never found it, though our wrists were spritzed silly and our nostrils soon clogged with all the bouquets cancelling themselves out. Then one day she comes in with "Lauren": spicy, not sweet or strong. For a long time the choice was "Tearose." I hate flowery smells, she now says. This is like nothing I have ever known. I smell citrus, spice. It took me so long to find. "Why did you give up on 'Tearose'?" "I hate it! It suddenly turned on me and got me sick." *Two men are seen, walking down a country lane in the evening, looking for work. They arrive at a farmhouse, where an old couple takes them in. They sit down to supper at a long oak table. One man tells the old couple a secret, just before the meal begins. He points slowly across the table-top. He talks low. "He," he starts, then stops. "He … is … dead." The other, older man holds out his arm for them to see. They all watch the gray hairs on the white skin rise, and stand on end.* On the phone: "I like to share the kitchen experience." She who never cooks. This is a version of the self for one she's decided to take into her confidence. "I want a lover/Who won't blow my cover," she'd quoted me. I can tell a lot about her phone companions: "I used to be political in the sixties. Even the seventies. I went to a party protesting events in El Salvador. The people there were political because they didn't have anything else to do." She doesn't smoke, but on the phone she lights up and puffs like an old film star. She is someone I don't know. I'll see if it's her. When she gets off the phone: "Would you like to go to Israel this summer?" She'd often talked about Jewish heritage and stuff. "I hate Israel! The asshole of the world! You should have heard what Jules Feiffer said about it!" A couple of years before, I had attacked Israeli policies. She'd screamed, and locked herself in the closet, yelling I was an anti-Semite…. In the morning she puts on David Bowie's "In the Port of Amsterdam," off the *RARE* album. "There's always something a person wants to do," she says. The present moment sustains; moment lost through habit or indifference. She sitting in her chair by the window. The photos of her father over her head, surrounded by books to the ceiling. A mug of coffee on the desk beside her. She is wearing her morning-coat, open at the throat so I can see the creases down her chest between her breasts. A pen dangles from her fingers as she pauses in marking up newspapers. Public Relations is always looking for angles. Pens without tops are strewn all over the place. Inkstains everywhere. Newsprinters ink is worked into the white edges of doors and round the handles. Coffee she drinks scalding, but leaves some which she drinks cold. It is in the fat cup I bought her, her most recent favorite. But the last ten cups of coffee, she says, have been bad. But then again, everything changes. Yes, it is her.

Lem Has a Problem

I have always existed in dream time, in a wash of evocations. I can't escape into consciousness. I'm in the grip of something that does not want me…. And now a rabbit is in the bath, fur stripped except for the tuft; all ribcage. So vulnerable, so white inside the porcelain rim, like sugar. And I can't locate in her all I say she's caused. It doesn't have anything to do with her. It is autonomous. Or seems to have drifted like a net from me, an impersonal history. She in the tub cannot be the cause. I cannot be effect. It is too large. This must all have happened somewhere before, somewhere else, *in illo tempore,* to someone else who is now remembering it, and so is more than hypothesis.

HE CAN'T BE SERIOUS FOR LONG

This is emic *and* etic, this small *tristes domestiques,* this fieldwork in commonplace, on ordinary illness. This is postmodern ethnography, privileging discourse over text, dialogue over monologue, collaboration over the ideology of transcendental observer, since there's "nothing observed and no one who is observer" (Stephen Tyler sounding like a Sutra). It is "fragmentary" and not a "self-perfecting discourse." It's part of an "emergent mind with no one locus but an infinity of possible loci," (oh, Indra!) It's polyphonic "fantasy reality": where is the object, where the subject? At least, that is what I'd like it to be. Perhaps Novalis said it best: Every illness is a musical problem which requires a musical solution. Science has failed, yes, but it makes for good stories; some things are better to believe than others. By middle age you need new ones, sure, but it's still amusing to see Freud, the depressive who took cocaine, mapping out depression for the first time as grief over a lost object, and writing that anger + grief = melancholy (repressed hostility) (or also hostility is depression viewed in terms of cannibalistic tendencies of the oral-sadistic phase in the libido's development). Which reminds me of a story I once heard about a friend who paid a hundred bucks for a seal-point, who, it soon turned out, ate anything made of wool. Once her fifteen-year-old daughter took off her sweater when she went to the bathroom and left it over a chair—"oh, just for five minutes!" When she came out, half had been devoured. They hung up their coats in the hall, and all the cuffs were

sheared off. Any socks left about were ingested. Even material that was only wool-*like*, that was all eaten up. It seems that the woman they bought the kitten from had let it play with her husband's socks. This fixated the beast on something mother-like, comforting and warm. And so it embarked upon a career of matriphage. Luckily, just as my friend was about to leave for a trip to Europe, the woman she'd bought the cat from called to ask if she would sell it back, her daughter missed it so. My friend, pretending reluctance, asked the same price she'd paid. The woman threw in ten bucks more because the cat had grown so big. And everyone lived happily, etc.

LEM HAS HIS BIRTHDAY PARTY CURTAILED

She cannot travel by plane. At Heathrow she was out. On the limo's back seat she nuzzled against my arm as we drove through the damp night north, while the smoke of burning stubble sank into everything, a smell I'd forgotten over the years. I love travelling with her. She is my family where I never considered I'd ever had one. My father had been a fearsome presence I'd spent my whole life trying to placate.... And now this trip to coincide with my birthday. It was a hot summer, like something out of pre-history, or when grapes grew here and Anglo-Saxons picked them to make wine. My birthday was ninety and rising. The little old ladies from across the street and my old Aunt Vi from Fordham were sitting beside the lawn and sipping. Sunday. Quiet in the trees and on the grass. The clock slipped by to five. Where were my sister, and her husband, he who'd cycled round the world in his youth and now went to old folks' homes and impressed them with his slides? (When my sister was pregnant, each time he'd made her ride to the hospital.) And where were the kids; one, a bright girl of ten, the other a candy-gorging boy of six, and the three-year-

55

old whose hair was filthy and full of lice? They'd gone the day before to Clacton-by-the-Sea. They'd said they'd be back. Three hours there by train, a couple of hours sitting on pebbles, then three hours home. They'd asked if we wanted to go. If we're not at the station by eight then leave, I said. I didn't realize they'd planned it in my honor. Well. All that afternoon, as on every other afternoon, my mother complained of—let's call him Bill. Lazy, he was, and hadn't done a thing to the house ("which your father bought them."); he's bike-mad, mean too. Won't put in a phone or buy a car, "but he'll take them both if I pay." All he wants is her money, and so on. "Oh, *please,* Lilian," S moaned, "please lay off! Can't we talk about something else?" My mother pulled herself up and put on what she thought was an aristocratic bearing. "And just to who do you think you're talking to, young lady?" she postured. Words were exchanged and they parted, wife to the lawn and the old ladies, mother retreating deep inside her house, where we soon heard her at the typewriter. "That's her cutting us out of her will," I said to S. We laughed. We knew it was true. So I left on an old bike to scour the route for sister and brood. There they were, line astern with Bill leading the flotilla, kids riding in the middle, sister riding herd, the baby strapped behind her in its seat. My greeting brought a sick smile from Bill. The kids ignored me, staring straight ahead. From my sister ice. From the baby an exhibition of nose-picking and head-scratching. "So, did you have a good day yesterday?" I asked. Ice. Then, "We waited half-an-hour for you. We almost missed the train." "But—" She was now a smoldering one-seventy-five-pound volcano, whose anger almost sent her crashing into the bike in front. "We said we'd be there if ..." "Bill took the day off special. You just don't care about us." "But it was Saturday!" "You've always got the quick answer!" Oh hell, not all this again, I groaned. The cavalcade had now reached the house. It dismounted.

The two eldest kids got out their music and stands. Violin and recorder began a concert on the lawn. The old ladies sipped their tea, and kept filing off to the bathroom. Bucolic birthday on the grass. At first it was a roar. And then the locomotive rounded the bend, my sister, snakes in hair. She scattered all the little old ladies, knocked over cups and tables. The kids ran for the trees. "WHAT DID YOU SAY TO MY MOTHER!"— heading straight for S. "We don't want you here, you fat cow!" I looked around. Was she yelling at someone else? S is one-ten, five-five. The fists were up. The avalanche upon us, I stepped in front. Out of the corner of my eye, I saw returning churchgoers peering over the hedge, and I imagined their lips: "Those Greeks! Those Pakis!" They hurried on. "Just let me get at her!" called the voice at my back. "I'm from Brooklyn. I'll—" A fist smudged my ear. Bellowing "Big fat cow!" my sister made a rush I parried with an arm, tipping her, off balance, straight into my father's prize roses, white Peace, red Queen Elizabeths. She didn't fall, but left the footprints of a giant in the puffy soil. Then she started screaming at me. "You only came because my mother paid your fare! You hate us all! If you loved us you would never have left!" Twenty years ago I left. When my father died I suppose I was to have filled the gap. I once said to her: "Look, Dad's gone. But you have Bill." "He doesn't count," she'd answered, and walked away. And now she was charging through the roses, red, white, completely out of control. Any old ladies who'd crept back out now scuttled off again, into the house, terrified chickens. This time I had to slug her. But only on the shoulder. She spun off like a stricken aeroplane into the poor roses again. And sat down on poor Peace. Flash. My sister and I fighting as kids. I hurled a book that opened her eye. In a fury she threw anything that came to hand. I ran for it. Her long-headed skinny mate put in a piping-voice appearance. It was the first time I had seen him stand up to her (maybe because he could now stand over her). "Pull yourself together! You're making a fool of yourself!" He hauled her to her feet, and steered her like a broken bike to the gate. The kids came out quiet from the bushes, and climbed aboard. Then they all pedaled off in the direction whence they'd come. That was years ago. I haven't seen them since. The letters from the oldest girl soon stopped. Mine went unanswered. They forbid the kids from seeing their grandmother. They have told her they disapprove of her trips anywhere. They have given her to understand the money could be better used at home.

LEM GOES TO ANOTHER GREAT PARTY

"We'll leave at three, right? I've come in for my orders." "No. I don't want to walk that far in heels. We'll take the bus to the train." "*Ja, mein Führer!*" "That's what my mother used to call me. 'Little Hitler'. I wanted my own way always." "Well, thank *goodness* you've changed." Rain. The city's mad. And one must listen to madness. "I get all this electrical acupuncture treatment," he called out. "Turn it up! I've got a high pain tolerance. It ripped the skin off my kneecap. Rushed to hospital for tetanus shots. On a high bar I ripped my back muscle. Went to chiropractor. He's an idiot. Doesn't know what he's doing. By the time I'm finished with him I'm the cripple you see here now. I can only breathe out of one nostril. I was a bookkeeper. Can you spare some change? A dime? Anything? Thanks, buddy. Have a good Rosh Hashanah." The subway takes an hour. We walk warily under the scaffolding round the building that is supposed to protect from falling bricks. Men with prayer shawls wrapped in embroidered velvet bags run bent over through the rain. There is more Yiddish than English and more Russian than both. Her mother's ready; the table's set, ready to go. S can't eat. In ages she hasn't seen her sister

who says, "I'm proud of myself," time and again. She says she
has a Puerto Rican boyfriend who's teaching her how to make
beans and rice. He used to work at the Post Office. She stares
at S, reminds her when she used to have long hair "down to
here." She touches her hips. Her leg goes to sleep. Her mother's
friend calls her mother "dear," "darling," "honey," continually
for the guests. One of his eyes is closed and gummy. He's been
around almost since her father died. "Three thousand dollars
each, top plate and bottom," he announces, tucking in. "I've
got an umbrella for you," he says, not looking up. "That's very
nice," S's mother says, surprise in her voice. "I haven't had it
long—a few years. You can have it for three dollars." Part of his
mouth is numb. Food sticks all round.

And Stays There For a While

My flash picks out the small male toad clinging to the saddle of
the vast female: a motorcyclist trying to kick-start his engine,
or, having gotten it slowly rolling downhill, trying to wrestle it
into gear. I flick off my light. From the woods comes a shriek
like wheels skidding on wet pavement and hitting something.
The driver drives on.... She holds her sun-visor so illumination
strikes, eating her face. She is. Not anyone I know. Her eyes
go blank. Mine hurt. The sun goes in. Her face comes back.
The sun returns, and she is secret. What have I seen? Wife or
widow? Girl or woman? Here and there, gone and recovered,
one small shale hill at her back, fern, and flannel leaves of the
mullein framing. She holds up the visor like an illuminated
psalter, and sings without moving her mouth and ancient
unknown language of the sun.... All summer wells have gone
dry. Trees quit. Birds bounce on strings against clouds scorched
at the edges and curled back. And here I sit with a large bottle
cradled like a phone, flies like dogs, and wait for shadows of

Brian Swann

autumn on the floor like doorways leading down where rocks
are alive to reservoirs through which my voice will go on and
on like glass singing....

A Small Bug

fell out of a lightbulb onto his head, then onto the floor. It spun around on its back like a breakdancer. Eventually, it stopped, and lay still. He thought: he's done for. But the insect pulled itself together and soared back up, straight up, a Harrier jet. A few minutes later, repeat performance. He watched it spinning on its back, then crushed it under his naked heel.

That was the night before. Light was now billowing in the window, falling across a surreal landscape on an easel, and across the edge of an unfinished self-portrait. He walked to the door of the small, two-room adobe he'd rented, and opened it. He was glad to see, in the trees around the newly-turned field, more than one magpie, and what he thought might be a pair of pinyon jays, "blue crows." One magpie was bad luck. Clumps of cottonwood wool had piled everywhere. It even festooned other trees. He looked up against the blue sky, the sun rising halfway, and stretched as cotton blew off the massive tree like smoke, filling the air with barely moving puffs. When a stir of wind got among them, they swirled and swooped. Once on the ground, they piled up in small drifts, filling ruts and hollows in the crumbling clay. It was like winter in summer. He looked across the field to the house of his nearest neighbor, a man who, he'd heard, wrapped his semi-tame deer in reflective tape during the hunting season.

He'd come to enjoy these mornings of views through scruffy trees to small fields ploughed and sown with alfalfa, fields hedged in with great five-foot aster stems and their balls of fluffy seeds, magpies fishing the fields under the massive clumsy-looking nests they always stuck right in the middle of the trees. He liked the way the sun reflected off the world as if the world were made of copper.

He shivered, turned the change in his pocket, and recalled his grandmother telling him it was good luck at the full moon. But his pockets were getting lighter. He'd liked the odds at the time, but now he figured his pockets would be empty by fall. For the second time in two months he'd dreamed he'd just bought his mother's house, which was empty. She'd taken him out to dinner and stuck a big bill in the waiter's waistcoat pocket.

II

The house was surrounded by tumbleweed and sagebrush. A tall fence ran around the yard to exclude coyotes and other undesirables. He called out, but there was no response. So he opened the gate and went in. A terrier-size dog ran up, wagging its tail, then turned and resumed whatever it had been doing. A young turkey shot by, and then a small flock of pullets ran through his legs. Then more half-grown scaly-legged turkeys. He found himself watching the dog, running from place to place, nose to the ground. Snarf snarf here, snarf snarf there. Now and then it would find a candy, tear at the paper, swallow both candy and paper. The dog ran over to where he was standing and lapped up something just behind his left heel. He looked down. Small piles of turkey and chicken shit. The dog looked up at him, wagged its tail, and trotted off. "Anybody home?" He almost hoped nobody was. He sidestepped the birds running here and there like demented dinosaurs, hunting evening insects. In their panic, grasshoppers were hurling themselves against the adobe-plastered walls of the house. "Hi!" A long arm reached through an open window. "Be right out!"

Beside him, David felt tiny. Red Coues was a tad short of seven feet, grizzled ginger hair pulled back into a Willie Nelson braid. David had first met him at a bar off Route 68. Over a glass of lemonade, he'd told David how he arrived from Chicago in the '60s, joined a commune, married, and stayed. He'd published a book of poetry, and now worked part-time in a government-sponsored program for the pueblo. His wife taught part-time at the local highschool. "Only got one kidney," his voice boomed. "But that's no reason you shouldn't drink!" David took the glass with purple liquid. "Good to see you," Red said. He raised the glass in a brief toast. There were greasy fingerprints all over, but just over its rim, great galleon clouds were sailing over the Sangre de Cristo mountains, trailing dusk, catching the last of the sun. "Can't drink," said Red, "but I can toast you in a smoke!" He fished out a joint from his shirt pocket, and lit up. "To forget the day. Just joking." Molly, his wife, waved a sturdy arm from a window. A ghost full moon was visible just over the large silver water tank. "All ready for the one-acre development," Red wheezed. The moon was slowly turning a light blue, then pale purple. "She'll be out in a while. Putting the youngest to bed." A nighthawk flew over, screeching. "Nighthawk." Natural and supernatural with the self-same ring are wed, thought David, as a big tailless cat walked along the outside of the fence in the sage, dangling a prairie dog in its jaws. A collie-like dog ran from mound to mound. Red took a deep drag. "A neighbor poisoned the village a year ago. The colony of burrowing owls went with it. The dogs came back, but not the owls." He handed the joint to David, who shook his head. "Puritan?" "I, no— yes. A bit. Had a problem. But what the heck!" He took a drag. "Molly is almost sure she heard a flying saucer last night. She heard beep-beep noises behind the house, like nothing she'd ever heard before." Just at that moment, a naked baby with an erection ran from the house. The dog ran over and began licking the crawling, stumbling, wobbling child between his legs and buttocks. David went to push the dog away, but Red said, "The Indians say let the dog be with the baby. He never wears diapers. The dog cleans him and they'll be bonded for ever. It happened with our eldest, and she's at college." "That dog will never go hungry round here." They both stood watching the sky do great things in its opposite parts. The sun had finally melted, and the moon was acquiring a mad-dog look. "Lots of birds gone from the spruce-bud worm spring," Red muttered, just before Molly came out, and set off in pursuit of the baby who was in pursuit of the chickens.

Black beans with many homemade relishes and grilled jalapeno peppers were set out for the party. Though he was hungry, David had little appetite. He sat by the window and watched the dog. He picked at the peppers. A long hand glided across his plate. "Naomi," she said. He looked up, and then some. Her high heels made her even more impressive, as did her flounced Mexican skirts. "Dave Herbert," he replied. "Not hungry," she said. "I'll just pick." And did. From his plate. He glanced at her companion, who extended her hand. "Ethelou," she said slowly, pronouncing each syllable. "Bilagody." David stared at her, at her large eyes, wide apart, liquid as a deer's. She wore an elaborate and modern-looking necklace of turquoise and silver. "Yes, yes," he said. "Good to see you. How are you?" "Fine. How's your wife?" David's eyes had switched to Naomi, who had kicked off her heels and was stretching. Her hands almost touched the ceiling and its fake vigas. Then she walked to the back door, greeting Red and Molly as she passed. She sat down, reached into her pocket-book, drew out a joint, lit it, took a deep draw. Soon she was lying on her stomach across the door, asleep. "Her husband used to play for the Harlem Globetrotters," Ethelou explained. "I didn't know they played white men," David replied. "They don't." "Do you miss the east?" Ethelou inquired. "Miss? No. Maybe I'll stay here. If I can find work." He turned to Red, who had wandered over. "Do you?" "Miss it? No. I haven't been back in years—if you can call Chicago east." "He liked New York, though," Molly added, as she poured wine into David's glass. "He used to have friends in New York." There was a pause. "Tell him— it's a good story." She poked Red in the ribs. "Sure, sure," said Red, lighting up another joint, and passing it round. "I do have friends in New York. Ever heard of Johnny Machine and Rupert—he's a Chinese hood?" David shook his head, and took a toke, which Molly held. "I was meaning to ask," he coughed, "do you believe all those Indian things, you know, when you dance it rains, and if you tell stories in summer it'll snow? Ghosts, transformations, you know." "All I know is that those people have studied such things for thousands of years," Molly replied. "Why not ask Ethelou?" "I read a story the other day, in the library. 'The Man Who Married a Deer Woman.' He cheats and she knows. She just knows. He has to leave, and wanders, alone. Years later, he shoots a fawn and it turns out to be his own son. It sticks in the mind." "You should ask Ethelou," Molly repeated. "It's so easy to make a mistake." "Want to hear a joke?" Red asked. Before anyone could reply he said: "What's an Espanola vibrator?" "Is it a kind of Polish joke?" David inquired. "Give up? It's a beer bottle full of flies!" He choked. "New York friends," said Molly. "Whew," her husband wheezed. "New York friends? Oh, yea. Friends are important. So is family. Yeah ... There's Johnny Machine and Rupert. They insist on being my bodyguard every time I go to New York—Johnny was Mailer's when he ran for mayor. Or was that before your time? Hey—what's an Espanola vibrator?" "A beer bottle full of flies," David replied. Red stared at him for a while. Then he continued. "Yea, those guys ... I never told them when I was going to be in New York, but they always found out and insisted on being my bodyguard." He took a deep breath. "Are you a gambling man, DH?" He didn't wait for a reply. "You see, Johnny's a compulsive gambler, and you have to understand that. Once he was in Vegas and lost all his money. So he had to spend a week washing dishes." "More wine, Dave?" It was Ethelou. He held out his glass. "Thanks." "A whole week up to his elbows in greasy water! When he had enough money he decided to go back to New York, so he went to the bus station. But the bus was late. He wandered around inside a bit, and got the itch, but he'd really made up his mind. No gambling. He went outside for a breath of air—they've got gambling machines in the bus station, you know. They've got them everywhere in Vegas. Even on the buses. Anyhow, he goes outside—and gets robbed of all the money he's saved—did I tell you I have another friend in New York called Joe the Pipe? No? Well, just before he hits them, he says, 'Tell them it was Joe the Pipe.' Anyhoo … Johnny wakes up in the hospital, head swathed in bandages. And while he's lying there he hears some administrators talking about some money they're leaving overnight in the hospital safe. So, when the coast's clear, he gets out of bed carrying an empty pillowcase. He finds the safe, and has no trouble cracking it. He stuffs twenty thousand dollars into the pillowcase and starts back to his bed to plan how to get the stuff out. But first he has to find his clothes. He looks everywhere, in all the closets. Nothing, He starts prowling around outside, but the night nurse hears him and sends him back. So he decides to jump out the window, and then improvise. He jumps, and breaks both ankles—he's on the fourth floor. He finds himself in his nightshirt crawling down the road dragging the pillowcase. He sees a taxi and hails it. He tells the driver to take him to California, and pulls out a wad of notes from the pillowcase. In the taxi he passes out from the pain. He wakes up in the same hospital, sans pillowcase, sans everything. Everybody's talking about the safe robbery the previous night."

Red closed his eyes, smiling. David realized he was now sitting on the floor, next to Ethelou. Others were coming in, stepping over them, bringing various dishes. David was a little nauseous, dizzy. His mind jarred, seeming to stick on a long ditch. There were ruins of house-fronts along the ditch, which had once been a river in a valley. Something like the Via Appia. "It was the wrong address, right?" he murmured. "Yes," Ethelou replied. Out of the corner of his eye, he watched Naomi move from her belly onto her back, still lying across the door, like its guardian. She scratched her belly a slow scratch, eyes still closed. "She's exhausted," said Ethelou. "She runs the restaurant, almost all by herself. She's a great cook. And she's going to school part-time in Albuquerque." A memory rose in David's mind. The letter had been sent to the person who used to live in their apartment. His wife had opened it because she liked the handwriting and had invited the sender, who turned out to be Ethelou, to stay. She came to New York to get orders for her jewelry. It was only two months before Madeline had left her buyer's job at Macy's and run off, first with a woman who owned a toy factory in Brooklyn, and then with a lady copy-editor at Knopf twice her age and weight. Ethelou had arrived just when David was starting his third job in a month, working in the greenhouses at the Brooklyn Botanical Gardens. "How is your wife?" "Fine. She's fine, I think." Over his protests, while he watched, she had gone through Ethelou's suitcase. Packages of unopened condoms, three new diaphragms, a box of pills. On each of the four days of the visit, she had checked to see what, if anything, had been used. On the fourth day, he had pointed out spots of blood on the parquet floor, and a small pool. "I remember the dreams you told me." Dreams. Nightmares. Just one of the reasons his wife had given for leaving. "Yes," said David. "When we went out to that Greek place." "Yes," he repeated. "What was the name?" He thought hard. He couldn't remember, then— "Madeline!" "No. I mean the restaurant." "Oh, I don't remember." He became aware of her thin legs under her cotton skirt. Then he became aware of how thin all of her was, and long, but big boned, wide-shouldered. Coiled up. And, down to her hips, free-flowing, her raven-black hair. Noise from the record-player was making talking difficult. "The dreams. Houses," she continued. "Two and three stories: legs, trunk, head. A road leading along country lanes, and a future city there, penciled in, ghost lines. But no people." "Not worth remembering," said David, remembering. She stood up, casting a shadow over him. He stood up too. "And in the other, you said you had been involved in a killing, but not intimately. You said you'd left the dream with a query." "Yes, yes. I remember. 'If I am involved with evil, even if I have done evil, is my nature evil? Am I evil'?" "And you said the only answer would be, not an answer, but an embodiment, like a novel." Why had she needed three diaphragms? "You said you were looking for yesterday's snows before they fell," she added. They both laughed. "Did I also say, 'Only he who already understands can listen'?" "You did. Sounded like something you stole." "It was. I probably stole them all."

III

It was Saturday, a week later. She was bent over a soldering torch, and didn't hear him knock or see him enter. He stood, leaning against the doorframe after the long walk, unsure why he'd come, or if he really wanted to be where he was. But then he began to relish his invisibility, began to take in the place, itemize, indulge in an opportunism that felt illegal or immoral.

A blanket, squares and diamonds, ganado red, hung directly opposite him on the wooden wall. Along the wall, behind the bench where she was bent over, back to him, working, ring gauges hung from a large turnkey ring. Stuck in holders, pliers sat with steel jaws open, saurian, waiting. Scissors, files, saw blades, hammers, tweezers. A large rawhide-headed hammer lay puffy on the bench. All at once, he was aware the torch was off and she was watching him. "Prest-O-Lite," she intoned, pointing. "Silver sheets, twenty-two and twenty-four gauge. Combo bench pin, ring and bracelet, mandrel. Over there, male punch and female embossing die, twenty-four gauge wire, electric melting furnace, tufa mold for casting, dental investment for ditto, handy Flix, Epoxy, sulfuric acid, water." "My— my father had a workbench," David said. "He never let me touch it. He said I broke his tools. Really, they were always doing things to me. Once an awl stabbed me clean through the palm, here, and out the other side." He picked up a small round silver object. "What beautiful old buttons. Bells too—concha belts?" She nodded. "Today's my antique day. This is the jewelry I've lived by, ever since the Institute. What the white folk want. Free-form turquoises, squash-blossom necklaces." "I thought they were really pomegranates?" "Whatever. If you come tomorrow it's my own day. Jewelry they don't call 'Indian.' It's been selling too, ever since my return from the New York trip." She picked up a pair of open scissors from the hard-earth floor. A horse neighed outside. David turned his head but could see only the paddock and large shed. "I call him Westchester," Ethelou said. "I bought him a year ago with the first real dollars from that trip. Do you want some coffee?" She took off the goggles, which she had pushed up on her brow, and walked over to a corner bench on which an old coffeepot was percolating. David took the mug of coffee and followed Ethelou outside. "You like horses?" "I don't really know," he replied. "I think so." "You'll like this one. He's quite a character. Which was how I got him so cheap." She was wearing old jeans and a man's shirt. No jewelry. As they approached the shed, a large black billy goat sauntered out into the chilly sun. He lowered his head, looked up, and stood still, watching. Ethelou scratched between his horns, and shoved him aside, spilling some coffee. At first, David thought there were two horses, but then he saw dim reflections of himself and Ethelou. "What's that big mirror doing in there?" he asked. "In order to answer that, I have to tell you a story." She patted the horse on his rump, then, pushing up alongside him, stroked his neck and withers. David thought he had never seen so huge an animal. "Everybody tells stories round here," he said. "It holds back the action." "Stories are action. If you know how to listen to them." "Sorry. Go on." "From the moment I got him, when he was only half-grown, it was impossible to tether him in the stall. He'd pull and scream and his legs would keep moving the whole time. He was a crazy stall-walker. And then a stall-galloper, and there's not much room in here, as you can see. He kept damaging himself. Then one of my brothers said: He needs to be boxed in so he can't move. Then he'll get used to the place and calm down. You should try boxing him in with tires. Well, I couldn't think of anything better, and my brother's a college man so that's what we did. Next morning when I went out to inspect the results I found Westchester covered with tread marks, as if he'd been run over by trucks dozens of times. Then another brother came over. Maybe he's lonely, he told me. Maybe all he needs is a companion. I've got this ram that spends his time eating the wool off his own back. Put these two nuts in with one another and maybe something will work out. So, as you guessed, we put the ram in, with much pushing and shoving, and hoped for the best. When I went out the next morning everything was quiet. Too quiet. But the horse wasn't doing anything crazy, and though the ram had eaten himself bare, things seemed as if they might work out. But by the following day they were both running in tight circles round the corral. So—can you guess?" "Another brother?" "That's right. My eldest brother, Yaz—he's an engineer at Four Corners. He said that maybe the crazy horse didn't like his name. So without consulting me he changed it to Bilagaana." "What's that mean?" "Well, something to do with his color. He also decided we should paint the stall pink, since he'd heard somewhere that pink was a good color for calming people down. He said that was why they used it in nurseries. So, we painted the stall pink and took out the ram. But it only seemed to make Bilagaana run in tighter, faster circles round the corral. So we repainted the stall white and put the ram back in. I should have known better, but maybe I was desperate. Anyhow, when Yaz suggested that a mirror might help I didn't say no. It seemed to make some sort of nutty sense. 'With a mirror,' Yaz said, 'the ram will think he's part of a herd, a small herd, sure. But he's not alone. And the horse will think he has a horse buddy too. I think they're running in circles, my wise brother said, because they're lonely and upset. They're trying to reach the herd, maybe, catch up, you know. Kinda catch themselves.' So, off we drove into town and went into the hardware store where we bought the biggest mirror they had, and we screwed and hammered it into that old gray wood stall there. The results you can see." "All seems calm," David ventured. "Well, it is. And it will be even better when either of them can break free of his own image. The ram's doing a better job of it. But Westchester's not doing so badly, either. I have hopes." "He's a beautiful animal. What are those dots?" "He's part Appaloosa—that's an Indian horse. I was also told he's part slow racehorse." "Is he a stallion?" "Gelding."

David watched a cloud of dust take the shape of a shiny pick-up. It pulled up, dust curling round its wheels, waiting for them to come out of the corral. The driver got out, and then the two men in back hopped over the side. They all wore Levi jeans, western boots, shirts open at the neck, and bandannas. The tallest one wore a bolo tie. David closed the corral gate behind him. They nodded in his direction and smiled at Ethelou. She introduced them. "Yaz, Billie, and Kee," she said. "David." They seemed a little unsteady to David. All shook hands. "From New York," she added. "Got any coffee, sis?" Yaz asked. "Damn," she said. "I just used the last can." David felt self-conscious. He knew it was unfair to blame Ethelou for making him feel uneasy. "I'll go," he volunteered. "How far is the store?" "Farther than you can walk," Ethelou told him. "OK, then," Yaz said, "We'll go get some." "Can I come with you?" Yaz looked at David. "OK. Hop up back." He sat between Billie and Kee, wiry young men. No one spoke. To break the tension, David asked, "Where you guys from?" "Near Shiprock." The roar of the engine being gunned almost drowned Billie's reply. Then radio yodels and twangs drifted back from the cab's open windows, and they picked up speed. David dropped his head back and closed his eyes. Doesn't this truck have more than one gear? he thought. "From New York," said Kee. "Excuse me?" "One of Ethelou's New York *friends*." David was unsure if this was a question, needing a reply. So he remained silent.

After an eternity of bumps and squeaks, they came to a halt. The driving had been erratic, at best. David was rubbing his back when his companions leapt overboard. They were at a kind of large roadside stand. David levered himself up and over. By the time he got inside, Yaz and Billie had already selected a loaf of bread, a carton of milk, two six-packs. Kee had chosen some Fritos and Doritos and other junk food. Each had a can of Hills Brothers coffee. David offered money, but they wouldn't take it. It seemed to David that they didn't like him. He put it down to cultural difference. Just as they were pocketing their change from the cashier, Kee dashed off and came back with a bunch of bananas. He held them in front of David. "What's these?" he asked. "Those? Why, bananas, of course." David was uneasy. Was he being taken for a ride? When he got outside they were talking. At his approach they all got on board. Yaz gunned the engine. Kee and Billie made themselves comfortable. David just sat. To his surprise, they began asking him questions: Where he was from, how he met Ethelou, what he did for a living, and so on. David fed them bits and pieces. When he paused they asked for more. It was some time before he realized they'd overshot the turnoff to Ethelou's place. He mentioned the fact to Billie. "Shortcut," he was told. But it seemed to be taking longer. "Fritos?" Kee offered. Light was shining at a strange angle across Billie's face, and for a moment David saw the face of the child he'd been told about. His mother had opened the door to a total stranger. She had the baby in her arms. His face received the full force of a vial of acid. A Vietnam vet, recently released from a mental hospital. "OK, then. How about a Twinkie?" "Oh, I'm sorry," David replied. "No thanks."

"Going to try one of these here *bananas,*" Kee announced, and tore one from the bunch. David could have stopped him, but instead he watched as Kee bit into the fruit, skin and all, just at the moment when the truck slowed down to turn a sharp curve and enter a tunnel. When they emerged, Billie asked his brother how it was, the *banana.* Kee didn't reply. He just sat there, bandanna and hair flying out, half a banana in his hand, looking kind of frozen. "What's the matter?" David asked. "Are you all right?" There was a slight movement across Kee's face. He blinked, then spoke. "Don't ever eat those *bananas,*" he announced, looking down at his fist. "I just took a couple of bites and I blacked out." Long pause. "Powerful stuff. Wait till I tell them back on the res." Another pause. "Drugs. They're drugs. No wonder you white folks have a problem. They're selling these *bananas* to anyone. Right by the side of the road. Anyone can buy them. One bite and I blacked out. No wonder your society is crumbling and coming apart. Everybody stealing. Everybody killing. How long was I out?" "Oh," his brother said, "couple minutes, at most." "They'll watch the Wheaties commercial different after I tell them this. The one when this guy slices a *banana* into a bowl of Wheaties and milk and sugar—sugar'll kill you too. Crazy white man!" They both burst out laughing, so loud that Yaz stuck his head out the window and glanced back at them. Kee peeled another banana and took a large bite. "Here, man, have one!" David shoved the bunch away. The truck slipped out of second, slid through the gears, and sailed on smoothly. The swaying and poor steering disappeared also. No one spoke.

IV

Naomi's restaurant was behind an adobe church, rather a famous adobe church. David thought he remembered it from one of his (uncompleted) architecture history courses from years before. Between church and restaurant was a drive-in liquor store. Red had told him that the local Democratic party chief owned it. David found it hard to concentrate on dinner as cars, trucks, pickups glared their headlights into the window, keeping up a steady stream. Most of the pickups had a gun-rack with at least one gun in it. Sometimes whole families would drive up and order, as if picking up candy for a picnic. New Mexico had the highest DUI rate in the whole country, Red had told him. David was about to inform everyone that he found the whole thing criminal, but he paused. He laid down the forkful of green chili. He was remembering a dream in which he was accused by a fat boy of a horrible crime. The boy had stolen his umbrella. At the trial, David had defended himself so successfully that not only had he convinced the jury that he could not possibly have committed the crime, but had gotten enough on the judge and prosecutor to send them away for life. He smiled, then. "Excuse me?" he said. "I said I used to do freeze-dry pets." It was Naomi. Business was slow, so she'd left her restaurant with the help, and come out with them. "I don't understand." "You asked me what I did before this." "I did?" "Yea. Freeze-dry pets. When they kicked off I kicked in." "Not such a step from freeze-dry pets to running a restaurant," David suggested. Naomi and Ethelou stared at him. "Joke. I'm sorry. Where was this?" "In LA," Ethelou answered for her friend. David cranked up some interest. "So why did you come here?" "Business wasn't good. I sold my business to the human sector for a perpetual viewing chapel. But I still put out this sheet where I tell subscribers how to freeze-dry their pets. And other stuff about animals." "That's nice," said David. "Nice? It can be life-threatening these days. Right now I'm practicing safe editing." "What's that?" "I'm not licking the return envelopes from San Francisco," said Kee who had hardly said a word through the entire meal. Then, just as everyone was getting ready to leave, he said: "Are you going to steal my sister and carry her off? Are you going to make an honest woman out of her?" David felt heat rising to his face. He stuck a fingernail into a thumb. But Kee hadn't waited for an answer. He and Naomi were standing, steadying each other. "Let us drive you home," Ethelou offered. "We can walk," Kee replied. He and Naomi started to walk with exaggerated attention to the mechanics of walking. "Shouldn't we make sure they're OK?" David asked. "Don't worry," Ethelou replied. "Her place is just ten minutes from here—if they turn round and go in the right direction. You know," she continued, "I

don't feel too good. Let's leave the truck here and walk a bit."
They walked round the church and up the dirt road. Dogs,
more used to four-wheel traffic, went crazy at the two-legged,
barking and snarling. But they were tied or chained to the
wooden fences so their reaction seemed more panic than threat.
Ethelou suggested a short-cut through a backyard. "Short-cut
to where?" David asked. "Your place," she answered. The yard
was slippery with the guts of pipe fittings and car parts, gutted
bodies, spiky with hacked trees and bushes. David's head began
to clear, and then he fell. He looked around and saw he was in
the middle of a small prairie-dog village within the town limits.
He got up, and brushed himself off. "Are you still looking for
a job?" Ethelou asked. "Maybe. It's very quiet." Light from a
growing moon was mixing with a few house lights. "It's not
because the beasts are asleep," Ethelou said. "Prairie dogs carry
rabies. The flea that causes bubonic plague was carried on the
rats that crossed the ocean with you guys. Everything was OK
before that." "Sorry. Sorry for everything. Sorry for breathing."
"A few months back, a kid shot a prairie dog, then played with
the body. He got bubonic plague. So they poisoned the whole
town. They missed two, however." "I think I live across there,"
David said, pointing over the little hillocks. He kicked at one.
"I go to watch them in that field on the way to the pueblo,"
he said. "They never look straight at you, always off to the
side." "Like Indians," Ethelou noted. "The little ones have a
great time, chugging along their little tracks in the grass. They
have beautiful Indian paintbrushes beside their burrows, as
if they'd planted them." "Maybe they did." "I hit one with a
stone yesterday," David admitted. "I think I killed it." "What
one earth did you do that for?" "I don't know. I just did." "I
don't believe you." "Please yourself." He stumbled again over
a hillock. Ethelou took him by the arm, to steady him. He
recoiled. "Aren't you chilly?" she asked. He colored at her

solicitation. "There are buffalo in that field too," he said. "I've never seen them." Ethelou did not reply. "I hear the old Indians could shoot an arrow clear through a running buffalo."

V

In the morning they'd driven to Santa Fe for art supplies. Just before they left, Ethelou said: "Stand over there. I'll take a photograph of you to show whoever you want to show it to when you get wherever it is you're going. Stand over there by the Archbishop." She had a large camera that would have looked more at home in an antique store than a large tourist plaza. The sun was in David's eyes as he set about obliging her. Under shaded brows, he watched as, f-stops and such at the ready, she raised the camera and aimed at the statue. Then she lowered the camera and looked about. She put it on the ground and stood with her hands on her hips, looking at David standing in a camera pose by the side of a rather puzzled, though cooperative, old priest. She walked over. "Excuse me, Father," she said, taking David's arm. "The *Archbishop!* The one death comes for. Haven't you read anything?" David gave a big laugh. "Gotcha!" he said. Now she was calling out: "Inside leg! Inside leg!" But he couldn't get the logic. Summer days had shortened, and still he couldn't get the knack. Push with the inside leg and the horse goes outside. Outside, inside. When you wanted to go right you used the inside leg, when you—he didn't get it. It seemed somehow the left and right had become arbitrary. He was struck by the thought. Maybe his ex-wife had been right. They had never been able to travel anywhere by car. He'd drive, she'd navigate. "Left here!" she'd call out. And he'd turn left. "No, *left!*" she'd yell. "But I did turn left! Don't you know your left from your right?" "It depends," she'd reply. And there'd be another fight. But maybe she was right. Maybe it didn't matter.

77

It didn't. He was brought to by Ethelou's voice. "Don't let him do that!" She would not give up. When Bilagaana had proven unpeelable from his mirror, she'd borrowed an old black nag named Satanas. David was atop Satanas now. He should have kept him tight up against the perimeter of the practice circle Ethelou had laid out. Instead, the horse had drifted into the middle where he had come to a stop. David wished Ethelou would stop yelling out orders. It was like the army again. He gave Satanas a few contradictory heel-taps, and then some vicious kicks to the ribcage, but his head still stayed down among the greenish tumbleweed bushes. Suddenly, David was almost yanked off the saddle by one of the horse's vigorous headshakings. He had forgotten the admonition to hold the reins lightly, and instead had wrapped them round his wrists. At each downward pull of the head, David was pinioned flat along the animal's spine. Ethelou walked over, grabbed the horse's head, and jerked it up. "*You're* supposed to be in control, not the horse." "So it's all about control?" he replied. "You have no instincts." She set about extracting him from reins, stirrups, and the various leather straps that hung from the horse and which seemed to David deliberately placed to impede and injure. "Go round a few more times," Ethelou told him. From his height, David looked down. "Once more," he replied. "And then I'm calling it quits. I really don't like treating animals as mere vehicles. I like to treat them with respect. And I prefer to walk on my own two feet." He tapped his heels. To his surprise, Satanas moved in the right direction. David knew he wasn't telling the whole story. In one of the books he'd found at the bottom of his father's wardrobe, under three cartons of Winstons and Camels, was a volume devoted to unusual sexual practices in Arabia, or some other equally exotic place. In order to create adult eunuchs from captives and the like, he'd read that one of the more humane and spectacular methods was to tie a man naked onto the bare back of a horse and keep the animal running for hours, bouncing the poor fellow up and down on his privates and prostate until terrible damage was done. Then he was ready for a new and tamer life. After each of his instructional rides, David quietly and gingerly slipped his hand down between his legs to check for damage. At night, in the privacy of his bedroom, he'd check his prostate, though since he never previously concerned himself with that organ he couldn't tell if it was swollen or not. To take no chances, after each ride he'd sink his hind parts into a tub of cold water, until the numbness frightened him.

He did his circuit, got off the horse, took off the saddle, put it in the shed. The sun was setting behind him, and was throwing warm gules onto Ethelou's house, which he'd just finished painting. There was nothing more to do. It was time. As he walked toward the house, he heard Ethelou's voice. "You forgot these." David looked up and saw the sun full in her face, like a torch, obliterating features. "I have a joke," he said. "Want to hear it?" She didn't reply. "OK. Miss Jones kept a private school. Miss Brown kept a private school, and Miss … Bilagody kept a private school. What was the monkey doing sitting on a block of ice?" She dumped bridle, bit and reins at his feet. "Give up? Keeping his privates cool!"

VI

He was descending slowly on a swollen ankle, which he hoped he had not broken in the jump and fall. He crossed a meadow filled with the floating puffs of chicory and was soon among trees still smoldering along the trail. Some had burned into charcoal pillars with strange flutings. Night would fall soon, and the air was still smoke-heavy. A surreal landscape. It was getting cold, too, and felt as if it might snow. He wasn't sure, but he might have gotten lost, and he hadn't bothered to pack a trail map. He continued through the burning forest. It began to feel like walking through a village just torched and plundered. Just two weeks in Vietnam, the last year of the war, he'd walked through the first of a number of such villages. A month later he was invalided back to the States.

His boots dropped a couple of inches through a pane of thin ice. A flame flared close by, in front. He looked down, where black earth under the ice gave back something like his reflection, vague warped streaks. He bent over, staring. Then straightened, stood silent, listened. Everywhere was quiet, serene, broken only by the crackling of a burning twig. No living thing within miles of all this, David said to himself. Nothing. But, as he found the sentence, he sensed something. He flicked his flashlight on, then off. He slipped his backpack off, and laid it on the ground. He felt a snowflake burn on his cheek. He was suddenly aware of his skin, his vulnerable anonymous face. He wished he'd brought a gun. Quickly, he snapped his flashlight on again, and pointed it. Two luminous green reflections, then nothing. He lowered his arm. In the back-light of some continuing fires, and with the aid of what light still lingered in the west, he gradually made out, some fifteen feet away, a large beast. He stared as she stared at him. Her large ears followed each small click. Her body was sleek as a racehorse; not a muscle moved. And then her body strangely yielded to the woods, transformed into the woods, only to materialize again closer by or farther off. David's eyes were frequently confused in the play and flicker of shadow and fire over her body. The shape was never constant. He tried to fit it into his mind, hold onto it, make it his. Some words floated up: Beauty is the moment of transition. He raised his flashlight, then dropped it, as if the gesture was somehow obscene. The doe looked straight at him, and then, slowly, turned and walked back into the burning forest, lifting her delicate legs deliberately, and was soon lost.

CHERYL

When I went to pick her up in the Italian part of Brooklyn she was halfway up the drapes and hard to pull down. I packed her into a bag I'd brought, but all the way home on the subway she kept trying to escape and even managed to almost get herself free a couple of times. I pushed her back down like a jack-in-the box. I'd decided to call her Marilyn since she was blonde and blue-eyed. Later I renamed her Paul, after Paul Newman, when I discovered she was a he. He was quite a handful in the apartment. He hated being alone and sprayed all over when I left for work. He also ripped up all the furniture and chewed the potted plants. But he was also very loving, sleeping on my lap, purring under the lamp on my desk and even sleeping on top of my head at night. But when his spraying became a real problem I decided to have him face the knife. This provided its own problems in the form of urethral blockage, a disease that had taken off my previous toms and why I'd decided to go female.

*

I hadn't noticed her when I dropped Paul off, but she'd seen me and she was the one who phoned for me to pick him up. When I arrived at the animal hospital, the receptionist whispered that her friend liked me, thinking me "distinguished-looking." Along with the bill, she slipped me a piece of paper which I stuck in my coat pocket. When a couple of days later I got a phone call from someone identifying herself as "Cheryl from the animal clinic" it took some time for the penny to drop.

*

While I stood waiting outside Joe's, I realized I'd forgotten to ask her what she looked like. I found out when a tall young woman with high, bushy, curly hair ran up wearing a mangy fur coat. Hairs came off and stuck to my burberry when she gave me a big hug as if we were old friends. Dinner did not go too badly, though she kept looking about the large room, empty, as usual, except for the group of old men in the corner playing cards and Parcheesi. Until she asked me what was going on I didn't realize anything was. "Who's that in the photos along the walls?" she asked. I looked around. "Mussolini," I replied. "Il Duce. And that's Joe with him, I guess." In truth, I'd never paid the place much mind. I just came in from time to time for the quiet and the pasta fazool. She seemed nervous, spilling wine on the tablecloth, then asking for Coke or Pepsi. "I don't really like wine," she said. I realized this wasn't a good place to have brought her when she asked for mayonnaise to put on the spinach. She'd never eaten greens before, "not as such." Her diet probably accounted for her rather poor complexion. We mostly talked about her, her job and abstruse animal facts, such as that rats and horses can't vomit. She said she was always surprised by the delicacy of a woman's bones and that sperm seems to open cracks in her tongue. After dinner, she took my arm, rubbing off more of her coat, and we walked through the Village, where she pointed out all the animals she'd cared for. "That dog nearly died. Now look at it. That's a vicious little mongrel, and his owner isn't much better. That Afghan ran off and had its cranium split open by a car. Howard wasn't in when the girl brought him by and she had no money so I gave her some to take a cab to another vet, the dog wasn't even hers, she'd been sitting it and when the owner came back he gave her a tongue-lashing and told her to take the dog back.

He said he wanted 'a whole animal'. Can you believe it? And there was the poor thing walking about with its brain exposed. Howard patched him up, and I paid for it. I'm still paying." Howard, she told me, was her boss. At first he was her "dream-doctor," what with "the white coat and blood spots, you know." Then she listed all her favorite movies, starting with *Gone With the Wind,* which she found romantic and sexy. She also told me how important books were to her, and how they'd had influenced her. For instance, she had never masturbated before she read *The Sensuous Woman,* she said. She also liked the theater and had just seen *Let My People Come.* She told me her first girlfriend had been a much older schoolteacher in Ecuador who had run off with one of her female students and been fired, so she joined the guerrillas and was killed.

*

Cheryl wore the same fur coat all the time. When I joked about its possible origins she got upset and added a suede coat to her wardrobe. Its orange dye stained everything it came into contact with, including me. I said I'd like to buy her a new coat for her 23rd birthday. "It's not for another six months," she said, and declined the offer. "I have all I need. Why don't you take care of yourself properly, and Paul?" Bending over the litter tray, "What's this?" she said, holding up crumpled pages of *Playgirl.* "No wonder he gets sick. You should only use kitty litter." Then she pointed to the crucifix on the mantel. "You should take that down when I come over. You know it gives me the creeps. What do you use it for? Vampires?" "I told you, it was my mother's." "Well, it gives me a headache. Where's your Advil?" I pointed to the bathroom. When she returned she looked a bit quizzical. "Why do you use vitamin E? An aphrodisiac? You got problems?" "What? No. I read an article on how it makes you live longer." "In *Playgirl?*" "No." "Why are you worried about that? You're not that old." "You said I was distinguished-looking." "You are, but you should lose that moustache. It tickles, and it looks as if you're hiding behind it." "There's nothing to hide. I lead a dull life." "You are a quiet one. Very quiet for a lawyer." "I'm not that kind of lawyer." "Lucky for you you're sweet. I don't come across many sweet guys. I wasn't sure at first how long this would last. I thought I'd hit bottom when you took me to see that movie, last year in something." "Marienbad," I said. "I could have screamed. And then I was sure it would end badly when I went face to face with an uncircumcised penis. I'd never seen one before. 'Now what do I do with this?' I said to myself. 'How do I find the hot spot? Where is everything?'" "You soon found out." "Yes, peek-a-boo, and that little cup holds all sorts of things. How did you escape the knife?" "Like father like son, I guess." "I wonder how your mother liked it." "Where they came from, baby boys weren't mutilated." "Well, it's quite a novelty here, believe me. Is it true men like them?" "How would I know? Isn't it the biggest you've ever seen?" "I've seen bigger. It's fun-size. So, tell me a secret." "I told you, I don't have any." "Tell me about your parents." "They were both killed in a car crash soon after they arrived in the U.S. I was a baby." "I don't believe you." "I don't blame you." "You don't have a foreign name." "They changed it." "Don't make fun of me." "OK, I'll tell you a secret when you get back from Florida." "Good. Maybe it's you have a three-way fantasy. Or you can tell me about your girlfriends, if you've had any. Or that you're gay." "Yes, I have, and no, I am not. I find that rather disgusting." "How do you know if you've never tried it?"

*

Cheryl spent Christmas week in Miami with her mother, who had married a dentist, "a dirty old bastard," she'd told me. "A pillar of the synagogue who stuck his hand up my skirt the first time he met me. I yelled at him and threatened to tell my mother. I got a free cleaning and two fillings out of him before I let him off the hook." To pass time when she was away I went to the Anthology Film Archives. It was boring. I was beginning to miss her when she phoned to say she had to stay a few extra days. During that time, Paul got sick again and Howard's place was closed while he was on his ski-trip. So I took him to a place that specialized in cats. A tall woman opened the door and waved me to a chair. "What's your sign?" she asked. "My sign?" "Your astrological sign." "No idea." "Well I can't work if I don't know your cat's sign." "Sorry." "But you must know when he was born." "Well, I picked him up in Brooklyn when he was about six or seven weeks old." "Not good enough," she said. I made something up and left Paul overnight. When I picked him up he seemed to mope a bit, and I did too but perked up when I got a phone call from Cheryl. She kept me on the line with stories, including one about the Tom Jones concert she went to with her mother who focused her binoculars on the singer's crotch. "'Look there, look there, Cheryl!' she yelled. I looked hard. 'He stuffs,' I told her. 'And he's gay. So are your other favorites, the two Burts, Reynolds and Lancaster.' That really pissed her off. Serves her right."

*

When she got back to Brooklyn it was to discover that her cat Gerald had died. She hadn't liked Gerald from the first and just before she'd left she'd hissed, "Gerald, I hate you." She cried when she told me the details. "You should always be honest with your cat, Al. Or perhaps you shouldn't. They can tell, and though they said Gerald died of a blood disease and couldn't breathe, I feel guilty. He had a sad life. I took him in after Howard had him shipped from California believing that since he was a Himalayan he'd be a status symbol and do things to attract the ladies, like walking at the end of a leash. But as soon as the crate arrived, Howard didn't like the way he looked and wanted to ship him back. I told him no way, and then he said he would put the cat to sleep. I couldn't allow him to play God so I took him home to Brooklyn. He was sick all the time and I had to borrow money for his treatment. Poor Gerald. I didn't really hate him. I hope he knew that." She kept crying until, "Pull your tits together, girl!" she said. To distract her, I asked how she'd coped with her step-father this time. "He was disgusting. I threatened to tell my mother but she probably knows already. He tried to persuade me to wear her high heels and step on his balls saying 'This is as close as you're ever getting to *my* pussy.'"

*

She jumped out of bed because she remembered a woman had an early appointment for her poodle. Cheryl was having to cover for Howard, who had been coming in late because of his new evening side-job as decoy at Caesar's Palace massage parlor, checking on the girls to make sure they weren't hustling. For his pains he got free turns. But by the time Cheryl got to the hospital there was no poodle but an angry note was stuck to the door. Over dinner, she said, "the bitch works with retarded kids. The ones with social consciences are the worst. And because Howard balled this one once she's even nastier. He apologized to the cow and took $20 off the bill. I wish he'd stop balling them. We can't afford his sex habits."

*

One lovely March day I dropped by to take her out to lunch in Washington Square Park "You know, Al," she said as we finished and picked up our litter, "you look better without that

moustache but you're still a strange person. You don't say much."
"Someone I knew used to call me 'a shrinking violent.'" "You've
probably got a lot of secrets. You promised me one." "You're
the interesting one," I said. "Let's go." Just as I was about to
drop her off, "Oh no," she said, "it's that old fool again, always
without an appointment. Last time he came in with a dog at
the end of a very rusty chain. It had been there for twelve years,
the time they'd lived together and the old fart was too scared
of the beast to take it off. Howard had to drug the animal so
he could get close enough to take the chain off and examine it.
There was nothing wrong. Healthy as rain. Let's use the back
door." We passed stacks of cages with animals of various kinds
inside. I stopped in front of a cage that contained a huge black
cat. It hissed at me. "What's that?" "That's Crunch." "Strange
name," I said. "How come?" "He's named for what he does.
We can't get near him. We phoned the owner to come and
hold him but he couldn't understand our problem with his cat
named 'Crunch.'"

In the waiting room sat a woman all in little-girl pink with
pink bows in her hair, and a pronounced Adam's apple. Her
miniature poodle had pink bows too, and was dyed pink.
Cheryl was suddenly all business. "Name, please." "Anytime."
"How about now? Name please." "Anytime." "What do you
mean, anytime?" "You asked my name. That's my name.
Anytime. Annie Anytime" "OK. Now what happens to be the
matter with your dog?" Annie tucked the animal under its tail.
"Anal glands," she whispered hoarsely. "Disgusting things,"
said Cheryl. Then, turning to me, "I used to do them, but no
more. I make Howard do them. After he sprayed me a couple
of times I made him point the dog the other way. He still gets
it all over the walls."

*

"Do I scare you, Al?" she asked. "A bit? Do women scare you?"
"Scare? No, well ... confuse, maybe. I've never met anyone like
you before. Why do you ask?" "No reason. We're very different.
That's a good thing, right?" "I don't know. You yourself called
me an 'alter kocker.'" "I was joking. You're really not that old.
And you're a *gentleman.* You're distinguished. You're nice to
me. You don't give me no grief." "You're easy to be nice to."
Which was true, though recently my work had been suffering
a bit. I'd been called out a couple of times and suffered a few
looks at the water cooler when my shirt collar couldn't cover
all the hickies. One vulgarian even mock-whispered, "Hey,
looks like Al got some last night." Though I'd worked there
quite a few years I was not on first-name basis with anyone and
nobody was on a first-name basis with me, perhaps because
they couldn't pronounce "Aloysius," or couldn't be bothered
to make the effort. They knew "Al" irritated me, so that's what
they called me.

*

Though she'd lived in New York all her life, Brooklyn born
and bred, the city was still full of wonders for Cheryl, a cabinet
of curiosities. There was, for instance, the man her gay friend
Tim told her about whose twelve-inch penis needed so much
blood to fill it up, every time he got an erection he fainted.
And she herself provided wonders for others, including me.
Like the time she ran across the street by the clinic, threw open
her orange coat, lifted her blouse and, braless, "Look, Al," she
called, as she dodged honking cars, giving them the finger,
"don't they look nice?"

*

I didn't see Cheryl for a while. "Been busy," she said when I called. "I was coming over a few days ago to surprise you, did my body, perfumed it, clipped my bush, but Howard made me work late. I felt like screaming. How you been?" "Me, oh, OK. You?" "Been to the gyn," she said. "Anything wrong?" "No, not really. But I got a new doc after the last one. He said, 'Cheryl, I almost don't know what you look like. All I ever see of you is down there.'" "Cheeky beggar." "Yes, well I thought I had VD last week so a friend referred me to another doc. I went in and he told me to strip. No formalities, Just 'strip.' So I did, and he felt my groin. 'Nodes,' he said. 'What's that?' I asked. 'Your feet,' he said, and burst out laughing. I didn't get the joke. 'Put your clothes on,' he said. 'I like you better that way.' And I hardly knew him, and all the time he'd been holding his knee against my crotch, like they all do. Only a few have nurses present, like they're supposed. Then he asks 'How often do you have sex?' as if anybody counts. 'Do you go with women? Does your boyfriend do you in the ass?' And I start stammering, 'Er, well, no, that's disgusting.' And then he starts lecturing me, how I was too young, and I start defending myself, though I never defend myself to anyone, not even my own mother, and he almost made me cry, and then I got angry and rushed out. I asked my friend if the doc was always like that and she said he was but she was used to it. Seems his daughter went to Europe last year and got the worst clap anyone had ever seen. Then she got pregnant and tried to abort by throwing herself down a flight of stairs. She worked in a shop and kept bumping against the cash register. Then she got trichomoniasis."

*

"You've got the common touch, Al," she said after I'd bought a newspaper and joked with the vendor. We were walking back to my place after seeing a George C. Scott movie, *The*

Savage is Loose. "You'd like my new friend," she said. "She's very quiet, like me—not. She comes into the office once a week to do volunteer work. She's the last person in the world you'd expect this of." "Expect what of?" "She told me she works in a massage parlor on 51st and 3rd. Howard must have visited and invited her down. Half-hour sessions, topless, in leotard. I was practicing last night when I guess it was you called but I couldn't answer because I was in my dancing slippers and tights and trying out new moves" "New moves?" "Seems a bell rings, 'Ting-ting.' If you haven't come, too bad. Just oils and powder. My step-bro said it wasn't for me, but I went up to have a look anyway. You can make hundreds." "I told you, if you need money—" "I'd even give Howard a freebie for putting me onto it if he ever came by. But maybe not. You know he puts animals to sleep then hides them in the garage. I find them covered with maggots. 'That's it, that's it,' I told him. 'Either you do it properly or I leave.' I'm working overtime now, but he doesn't pay me extra." "I told you—" "Thanks, but I'm fine."

*

Cold rain beat against my windows as we chatted. Despite the bad connection, I could hear it pinging against her windows too. She said her cousin was coming over later with some stag movies. Would I like to come by? I remembered Cheryl telling me about a cousin who worked at Macy's, and I'd seen a picture of her hanging onto a rope of one of the balloons at the Thanksgiving Day parade. Cheryl said she wanted to be an actress. They'd played doctor games as kids, and she'd described them to me. "Sure," I said. "Sounds interesting." I didn't tell her I'd never seen a stag movie. Now, Brooklyn was like a foreign country to me, and I'd never been to her place. I'd only visited the borough when I had to, to interview a client in a personal-injury case and the like. Still, I poured Paul some extra Kibbles and water and set off into the night. Somehow I found the right train, the F, and got off at the right elevated stop, the ominous-sounding Avenue X. I was pretty wet when I rang her bell. She buzzed me up and greeted me at her door with a hug and crotch grab. I looked behind her into the small apartment hoping to see the cousin in the photograph but all I saw was a young man setting up a screen and grinning, at me. "Hi," he said. I glanced around. "Where's your cousin?" I asked Cheryl. "There. Joel." "Joel? But—" Next thing I knew, I was dashing back along the corridor and down the stairs, Cheryl calling after me, "What's wrong? What's the matter?" But I was back out into the night, climbing the steps to the elevated station platform. When I got there I hid behind one of the pillars.

*

One spring day, Paul died. I found him on my bed. He was not even a year old. I called the veterinary office and asked for Cheryl. A male voice said "She doesn't work here anymore." I left it at that. Let the phone ring. I thought of getting another cat, but decided against it. I needed a break. Maybe Europe. Maybe anywhere.

When in Rome

" Si perecer, ven, caminante, a Roma."
"E ll'accidenti, crescheno 'ggni ggiorno."[1]

"Death destroys a man, but the idea of death saves him," said the lecturer at the British Council. "Tripe," said a voice to my side. "That's *Howard's End*. Up *Howard's End*. 'Only connect.' What shit. 'Such a crop of hay as never.' Such a crop of crap." "Ssh," whispered the woman beside him. "Mr. Traversi is a very spiritual man." "Half-dead, you mean?" "Well, *si*." "Then say so." I giggled. The man turned to me. "Dennis," he said, "and Fausta." Which led to drinks, which led to the job at FAO later that week. "Take the Metro to Mariana in EUR. Walk to the Fascist honeycomb building. Ask for me, or Colonel Viola." Which I did, since I'd just lost my job at the London School where Penny Heath had informed me that she didn't think I was the right person for the position. Her decision was not unexpected since I'd gotten off to a rocky start at the interview a month before when she'd caught me staring at her ample front. "Were you expecting someone else?" "Er, no." In fact Edward, one of my apartment-mates who she'd just fired, had described her as "a cow." I changed the subject. "Lovely office. Very feminine." She shot me a look. "I mean tidy." "My friend says that too. He's a colonel in the carabinieri. We run this

---

1 "*Si perecer, ven, caminante, a Roma …*," Rafael Alberti, *Roma, peligro para caminantes*. ("If you want to die, traveler, come to Rome").

"*E ll'accidenti, crescheno 'ggni ggiorno*," G.G. Belli, *Sonetti*. ("And mishaps grow every day").

place together. 'Feminine'? How horrid. My son, a mere boy, suggested I put up military prints. But I prefer those Cotswold cottages over there." "Factories would be more typical," I said, as sounds from the Trevi Fountain came through the open window. "Dark satanic mills. At least in my experience." "My father was a general. He stressed tidiness and order. But all my order is on the surface, I'm afraid. My drawers are a mess." "I beg your pardon?"

"Yes," she said, "I don't think you are the right person for the job. No doubt you're brilliant. Cambridge, was it, Oxford? But there have been some comments and complaints made by the young ladies under my care—" "Complaints?" "We needn't go into it." She caught me looking at her blouse. "Oh, I didn't realize I'd sat down with my blouse undone!" I thought of telling her that her colonel friend was screwing half the school but I felt bad for her and only said "With you, nervousness takes the form of belligerence." She agreed. "I'm sorry to let you go," she said, "but maybe I could find an hour or two for you, now and then." "No," I replied. " But thank you. I deserve to be fired. Things run their course." She crossed her legs, again. "Tomorrow to fresh fields and pastures new," I said, glad to let her down lightly. I was, as she said, overqualified, and teaching English grammar and idiom to Rome's spoiled youth held only so much charm.

*

A few days later, I found myself in the lush Third World, thanks to FAO, the UN's food and agriculture outfit, sitting in their luxurious cafeteria and listening to a little African at the next table saying "fear is the greatest spur," and a large German disagreeing. "No," he said, jaw muscles working like fists on steak and risotto, "food and drink. Drink not so much. Food." He took a swig of lager. His name was Walter, and he was dating the petite blonde Brit beside him, whose name was Judith. She said nothing as she fiddled with her salad, which she took out with her onto the balcony. I joined her. "Walter is from Wolfsburg," she said. "He worked in Volkswagen law." "I know," I replied. Soon she announced she had to go back to work. I followed her inside, where an American girl approached Walter's table selling calendars to bring spastics to the States. Walter took one and riffled through. "How much?" She told him. "For that I get three in Rome," he sniffed. "It's for charity," Judith pointed out. "Three I get," Walter said, dismissing the girl and waving over a rather tubby man whom he introduced as the next director, of what he didn't say. When he left, Walter complained that they'd promoted the tubby Madagascan for political reasons. "He cannot even speak English and does no work. Look at him. Ridiculous!" Judith departed for her secretary's desk. I held my tongue. I needed this job because Graham, another of my roommates at the Via del Tempio, he who had been "sent down" twice from Oxford, had just been fired from his English-teaching British Council job. It seemed that when he switched on his tape-recorder for the mostly-female class, what poured out was a stream of Italian filth which Graham accused Julio, his young live-in boyfriend, of putting there in one of his jealous fits. It was, in fact, recorded by Edward's friend, Gaea the poet, whose mother was a whore and whose father was a shepherd down from the hills. At thirty-five, Gaea was still a virgin, but got excited by little girls whose pictures he stuck up on his walls. He said in his plagiarized poems that he lived on "just coconuts and fish from the sea." Actually, he lived on money sent to buy him off by businessmen whose addresses he'd found in the phone book, and to whom he wrote day after day enclosing poems until they caved in on condition that he'd stop. He made a good living, he said, especially when he added prose to his arsenal, stories copied from obscure places which he passed off as his own. He hit gold when a man in real estate let him live in a vacant cliff-hanging house in the Alban hills. In return, all he had to do was write a novel featuring real-estate and a real-estate hero and come down to Rome each week to show the fruits of his labor. Slowly, surprisingly, Gaea was turning into a novelist, albeit one who still had enough time on his hands to play dirty tricks on his friends.

*

At FAO, it didn't take me long to get fed up with students never coming to class, preferring to spend time in their luxurious cafeteria, or shuttling back and forth between and among various countries; doing what, I never could find out. I spent a lot of time in the cafeteria myself. One day I saw Dennis there. He was, as usual, not in a good mood, his face dark, but I felt like complaining about my students, which I did until he interrupted. "Money for jam," he said. "Quit whining. My classes never turn up either. You expect too much of this place. Anything in Rome is a bloody mess. Just this morning I took the car in. Bent rod in the clutch. The idiot mechanic took a hammer and banged a whopping great hole in the side of the differential. '*Fa niente*,' he said when I protested. 'Then why,' I said, 'did they go to all the trouble of closing the whole thing in a nice box?' And now Fausta's angry with me because I got a letter from an old flame in the U.S., now married. She said she'd had a dream where she was Fausta. Fausta found it and flew into a rage. 'Why does she thank you for your *lovely letter?*' 'Lovely,' I said, in the sense of 'long,' or 'lengthy'? It didn't help. She's very jealous of *this*." He pointed to his chest. I must have looked puzzled. "Of *me*." He took off his glasses, wiped them, shook his loose gray hair as if to dislodge something. "Eight years with Fausta. I changed her life. She's no raving beauty, but sometimes, in the right light…. She would have been like her sister, hatched in a filing cabinet." He got up to leave, then sat down. "Did I ever tell you about how I forgot to bail the houseboat at Oxford and found myself reading Chaucer in a foot of water until the thing sank?" "You did. You know," I said, "you're a very popular teacher." "Some compensation for a wasted life," he said, getting up to leave. I was beginning to know what he meant.

*

"Do you still want that NATO job?" Dennis asked one evening in a ghetto trattoria. Before waiting for an answer, he was into a litany of his clashes with authority. "Rome's a putrid corpse," he announced, wine glass in hand. "But they're square with money," he conceded. "They have to be when there's so many documents and bloody bureaucrats." "Why don't you leave?" I asked. "I can't," he said. "He is still upset," said Fausta, "because Miss Mazzetti, you know her, she's in charge of English-teaching in all of Italy, was insulted by a remark he'd made. He said that all English teachers in Italy are incompetent." "I never said that," growled Dennis, "but they are. And then she asked me to phone that swine Traversi to remind him to turn up for his own lecture! Am I her slave? Then she asked me if I'd made the slides she said *she'd* made last week." "Calmati, caro," hushed Fausta, slowly pushing the wine carafe away from him. But he continued, ignoring her, pulling the carafe back. "She also said she planned to show some stupid BBC films for kids about fireworks and firemen. And then to cap it all she said that if that ghoul does not turn up for his own lecture could I step in. Me! A fall-back? No! And then she told me to make copies of some journals. I pointed out the existence of such a thing as copyright law, even in Italy." He sighed. "But I no longer give a fart!" "Ssh," Fausta whispered. "You're not in England now."

"Oh," he mocked. "I used a bad word. FART!" he bellowed. "I know some bad words too," Fausta threatened. To calm things down, I said, "Miss Mazzetti is afraid of you." Dennis snorted. "She asked if it would help to have an Italian stand beside me as I lectured to explain and answer questions. What, isn't my Italian good enough? It's better than her English. Talk about a *brutta figura*." "She's in love with you," Fausta ventured. "She wants her nephew there, that's all," Dennis continued. "Bloody intellectual incest. But I don't give a *fart!*" he announced again, looking at Fausta. "Maybe," I said, "she had Fausta in mind. She thought you'd want to cut her in." "Mm, could be. It's all so corrupt." He stared down at his untouched plate of carbonara. "Do you still want that job at NATO?"

*

I arrived at NATO Defense College one fine summer morning and found myself walking through the unmanned doors holding a nice green entry pass with my name and title on it ("Professore d'inglese"), a number (2193), and date (17.10. 67). A few weeks later, I saw Dennis in the lobby. He waved me over. "Rome's a putrid corpse," he said. "And good day to you too," I replied. "You think it's alive until you get up close and smell," he continued. "I think Joyce said that," I noted. Luckily the elevator was empty when he started in again with sagas of Roman malfeasance, beginning with the third degree they'd given him when they accused him of being a Communist because he wrote in *La Stampa* against the war in Vietnam. "The fools also accused me of attacking the British Royal Family. They got me confused with John Osborne. Do I even look like John Osborne?" We stepped out into a throng of uniforms. "How's your class?" "Working," I said. "Very funny," he said. "I mean—" "I know what you mean. They're a mixed lot. We don't really do anything. A Norwegian colonel told me they didn't need books, just conversation to help them at cocktail parties. And jokes. They insisted on jokes, arguing that dirty jokes were a great way to learn a language which, incidentally, they said they didn't need to learn because they knew it already. So, anyway, that's what we do, most of the time. Dirty jokes. They're just back from a couple of weeks in the U.S., where they picked up some really filthy stuff while at Expo, Houston, and Montana to see the missile silos. They also like to talk about spies, who they see everywhere, especially after I made the mistake of telling them I had a school friend named Paul Broda, who was the stepson of Klaus Fuchs, the atom spy. Paul's mother was the school's doctor who'd held our tiny balls and made us cough." "So," said Dennis, "it's going well." We split, Dennis to his class and I to mine, which had begun without me. A Norwegian captain was saying the Russians would attack his western shore if NATO didn't station forty trawlers there. "Russia wants to dominate the world," he said. "Like the US?" I piped up. Which got us to Vietnam and why I wasn't there. I escaped by a month, I told them, but they weren't convinced, though an Italian colonel said it was good discussing things with me because I was of the same generation as their sons. "I have no sons," muttered a Turkish colonel darkly, looking at the Greek captain. I was about to argue the case of Edward, my American apartment-mate on the run from 'Nam, but thought better of it.

*

I lasted two more months at NATO, after which I decided I'd had enough of war games, dirty jokes, tension between allies, and all the rest. The morning of the last day summed things up for me. We were in the middle of a French lieutenant-colonel's drone about the wisdom of De Gaulle when a beribboned and medallioned RAF air-marshal blundered into the room. "You chaps working in the dark?" "In the dark is right," I muttered.

"We find it more intimate." He glared, turned, and left just as Kraft, the German commander, resumed his diatribe about the litter on Italian beaches which he proclaimed "an international problem." "It was not like this before the war," he announced. I managed to change the subject but not before he'd told the class again about how in the Spanish Civil war he'd learned to love the bagpipes, and that he'd learned to play them. Would we like to hear? He reached under his desk. Luckily, the Greek captain and Turkish colonel had said something and were glaring at each other again. I wondered if the skirl of bagpipes might ease the tension, but decided against it. "Later, perhaps," I said. "After the jokes." The Turkish colonel got up and strode across the room where a Norwegian wing-commander was lamenting his country's vulnerability. The Dutch lieutenant joined him in his complaint. "Yes," said Kraft, "Holland. We did a little something there." I tried to calm the rising waters with a dirty joke about a Polish airman after the war who gave a lecture at an English girl's school, a joke which depended for effect on accents and the confusion between "Focker" and "fucker." This just made things worse, so I switched the topic to censorship, something they all agreed was good.

*

One evening not long after, I bumped into Judith in the Campo de' Fiori. "How's Walter?" I asked. "Would you like a coffee?" "He always says he's sick but he's fine. Yes. OK." We went into a bar and sat down. "Coffee?" "I'd really like a vitaminized drink." "Here?" She settled for a cappucino and began telling me about a horror movie she'd just seen starring a professor, his wife, and a robot. "The robot takes control of the car and the others have to kill him." "Kill a robot?" "Walter's got a new car. I'm not allowed to touch it. At Christmas we're going to Sicily. He's taking me, I think, because he still can't speak a word of Italian." "Great place," I said. "At least theoretically. I've never been there. But I've read *The Leopard*." "You could come with us." "I doubt it. And anyway I just got a new job with Esso Standard Italiana in EUR. They're sending me on a boondoggle up and down Italy testing the English of their employees. God knows why a truck-driver or a mechanic needs English. They're the only ones who'll turn up, to get the day off." "Good luck with that." "Money for jam." "You should get out while you can." "It's hard to leave Rome for the real world when Rome makes it so easy to stay. '*Roma te acecha, Roma te procura.*'" "What's that?" "Alberti." "I don't know him. In any case, you can't blame Rome for your own weaknesses. You should get out while you can. Or come to Sicily."

II

VISITATIONS

Noi siam venuti al luogo ov'io't ho detto
—Inferno, III

The noise of a plane flying low over the marsh shakes the window. "The food," Nora says to her daughter, "is still the exact equivalent of the religion: high in useless calories, full of preservatives, plentiful and bland. There's something eternal about it." "It seems pretty good to me," says Rose. "If I could have afforded—" I look at her. She stops. I've taken care of the bills from the beginning, though Rose pretends otherwise. Now I can afford someplace better for my mother, she won't leave. No point, she says. I haven't seen Rose for some time, but she is now thrice, twice our mother's size. The way she sits, slumped, round-shouldered, makes her seem even more massive. She holds a pocketbook the size of an encyclopedia on her lap. It keeps sliding off, and she keeps making elaborate and belabored movements of retrieval. Her husband, Stanley, thin, in a dark suit but no tie, says very little. He keeps looking nervously at Rose when he isn't reading aloud one of the many admonitions and prohibitions posted on the dining-room walls, squinting as he does so: "'Do not take more than you can eat.' 'It is better to share than waste. Jesus collected the leftovers.' 'Jesus recycles.'" "No vegetables. Processed cheese, instant coffee, canned juices," Mother says. "I'll soon be as fat as you." I'm not sure if she's referring to me or my sister. Rose makes a desperate grab for her pocketbook, but this time it escapes the clutching hand and lands with a thud on the floor, knocking over one of her aluminum crutches she'd balanced against the chair. Her husband retrieves the bag, and rebalances the crutch. She rummages carefully through the bag, making sure everything is still there. "Some people would give their hind teeth to be here," she says. "You're free, you're free to come and go. Nobody's at the gate." She ducks down under the table. When she gets back up, her face is the color of her retrieved lipstick, "Cinema Pink." "My heart," she says. "Stanley." "What is it this time?" her husband asks. "What's wrong with your heart?" "I've lost it." "You've—no you haven't. You're wearing it!" He points to her silver pendant. The dining-room manager clacks over in low high heels. She looks warily at Rose. "Is everything to your liking, Mrs. Wertenbaker?" she asks. Mother ignores her. Rose nods, smiling. Then glances at her watch. "What do you do with the leftovers?" I inquire. "There are no such things as leftovers," the manager replies, a smile forcing itself from her lips. She stands stiffly over us, staring down. Then she clacks off to welcome the guests at another table. "She thinks she's the maitre d' at a cordon bleu restaurant," says Mother, pushing her plate aside, hardly touched. From time to time she casts a glance at her daughter. Behind her, people are helping themselves to seconds and thirds from a bountiful table covered with a white tablecloth that falls to the floor all round. It is a magic table, never anything but full. Whenever a platter empties, one of the cooks, or their college-kid helpers, takes it into the kitchen and refills it. Sometimes, particularly in the case of fruit salad or corn, the kids reach under the table, locate a can, open it, and dump the contents into the receptacle. "Oh, fresh strawberries and cream!" exclaims one old lady, plunging the plastic dipper into the bowl of still-frozen fruit. Her middle-aged son drops some white substance onto the strawberries, and it sinks through the shining red liquid. "Great chicken!" The voice comes from the table next to ours. It is Harry. Mother turns and smiles. When she turns back there is a fresh plate in front of her: chicken reconstituted into an oval patty. She tilts back the top and the melted processed cheese looks back at her. "Kiev? Florentine?" she inquires of her daughter. But Rose is already drifting into her own thoughts. "What do you want I should have done? Left you in that house? You were rattling around, never went out. All you did was read. One day we'd have found you dead on the toilet. Is that a way to go? Is that a way to live? At least here you have your friends. I take care of you." "Rose!" Stanley exclaims, seeing things about to unravel. "Shut up! It's just not fair. I've got to do everything, and nobody thanks me. Pay for everything, take care of everybody. And me in my condition. What time is it?" She takes out a dainty handkerchief bordered with lace. A large 'R' is embroidered in one corner. She dabs it to her eyes and blows her nose. Then she tucks it back carefully into the left corner of her bulging bag. "Well, it's not! That— I won't mention his name, but you know of whom I speak—just ups and leaves, and I'm left with all the responsibilities. For all of you. And then when Daddy died, on the t—" It's all too much. The "of whom" of whom she spoke was our eldest brother, who joined the Army and got himself blown up in training. She makes a lurching movement and her pocketbook lands on the floor just at the moment when one of the navy planes drops a bomb on the offshore island used for target practice. I'm about to pick it up, but she grabs it up herself. "I wish I could bring him back! I loved him so. You had him all those years." Mother clearly doesn't want to provoke a scene like other times Rose was allowed to visit. But she says, "You have your husband." "It's not the same," snarls her daughter, regarding the retrieving back of Stanley. "Great chicken!" Harry calls across again. "It's Kiev!" Along the cloth-covered table, the festive towers of canned cranberry jelly are shivering on their plates. They appear for every meal, but on these once-a-month Saturdays there are more of them set out to welcome relatives. The United Church of Christ does nothing by halves. How Harry, who is Jewish, got into the place is anybody's guess. He has no relatives, and no visitors, and he doesn't seem to think there is any mystery. "Wasn't Christ a Jew?" he'd ask. "If this place is good enough for him, it's good enough for me. I never liked lox anyway, and bagels sit like a rock here." He'd punch below his ribs. Rose gets her crutches, and swings off to the bathroom. Harry moves across to her vacated seat. "How's your wife?" he asks me. "My—?" "Wonderful woman, your mother," he continues. "A dynamo for eighty-five." "In-law," Stanley corrects. "I wasn't talking to—whatever. Look, you're a man of some intelligence," he says to me. "Not too many here during the week, if you get my drift. All these predacious females. They never let a man alone. I'm from Sun City, you know. Retired there, but the women drove me out so I re-retired here." Mother sighs, and pushes her plate further from her, so it sits plumb in the middle of the table. Then she levers herself up and goes to the coffee urn. "Yes," he continues, "out there they outnumbered men ten to one. They're a real bunch of ambulance chasers, if you know what I mean. They watch the papers for obituaries, and when they locate a recently-bereaved gentleman—such as yours truly—they all rush over with casseroles and say, 'I was a friend of your poor recently departed. You must be in a lot of pain. I know how it is. Here, I've brought something for you to eat. And if there's anything else I can do for you, please don't hesitate to call on me.' And if you don't call by the time you've finished the casserole, they're back to collect the empty one and replace it with another. Ambulance chasers."

Rose comes back, all re-composed, repowdered, relipsticked, but more than slightly off, like a jello that's fallen to the floor and been scooped back together again. "Pull up a chair," says Harry. "I've got yours. All nice and warm it was too. Even round the edges." He pats the middle, laughs. Rose, scowling, pulls over Harry's chair from the other table, and lowers herself delicately, as close to the edge as she can. Nora returns. "Intelligence is a blessed commodity," Harry continues, addressing me. "Tell me, George—" "My name's not—" "Whatever. Which of these jockeys is *not*—I repeat *not*—a five-time Kentucky Derby winner?" Mother sighs. "Eddie Arcaro, Bill Hartack, Willie Shoemaker?" "I don't know," I say. "A man should know such things. How about the quarterback who has thrown most passes without an interception: Bart Starr, Bob Griese of the Dolphins, or Billy Kilmer? Stanley!" "I pass," says Stanley. "Hey, he's got a sense of humor! 'I pass!' What a guy! So—who? Stanley!" "Er, Bart Starr?" "Right! Now, one more, to show it wasn't a fluke." Rose says, "Stanley I want you to stop this nonsense, right this minute. We have matters to attend to." "Yeah, yeah," says Harry. "Don't get your bloomers in a twist. Relax." Rose glares at him. "I'm going to the powder room," she says, but doesn't move. "We should leave soon." "What baseball player's been hit the most times in his career? Dizzy Dean, Sal Bando, or Ron Hunt?" "I really—" "Take a guess. The right guess can show intelligence too, you know. There's intelligence in luck." "Sal Bando." "Close. Ron Hunt. Now, who was the first woman to drive in the Indy 500. Was it Kate Zartler, Rolla Vollstedt, or Janet Guthrie?" "I don't think it matters," Stanley mutters, watching Rose out of the corner of his eye, "who did or didn't." "Matters to them," Harry shoots back. "It was the high point of their career. You have to honor a person the high points of their career. Otherwise we're all the same." "Isn't that what democracy's all about?" I ask, for lack of anything better to say. "Facts and achievement, that's what interests me," Harry replies. "Especially facts. Gives you a grip on things. Where did Burt Reynolds play football? Who said 'nice guys finish last'? Who's the 'Galloping Ghost'?" "Galloping Ghost?" Stanley echoes. Then, "I don't think sports are important." "Everything's important, or nothing is," Harry replies. "Especially here, where everybody's crazy or half-dead—no offense." But Mother has already left, and Rose is staring straight ahead. When Mother is out of earshot, standing against the large window, looking over the marsh and the bay beyond, Harry leans across to Rose, who has been picking at her nails until they have started to bleed. "Fine woman, your mother. I don't know what she's doing in a funny farm like this. 'All the old folks at home.' Who wrote that song?" "Percy Grainger," says Stanley. Rose shoots him a look and pushes back her chair with a grating noise. It bumps into the long back of a tall man whose thick blondish hair is neatly combed back in a long sweep that ends at the end of his neck. "Sorry," Rose mumbles. "Nothing," says the man. She turns to look at him, watching him carefully until he turns the corner by the stairs, then she motions to Stanley to pick up her crutches. "Where's my bag?" He points to the floor. Harry gives a loud sniff. "Nazi," he says. "What?" Mother has returned with another cup of coffee in her hand. "Him." He indicates a man by himself on the sofa, reading. Mother turns and walks back to the window. Harry lowers his head and in a low voice says, "He showed me a novel when he first got here—in manuscript, natch. About the war in the Atlantic. Said it's all made up. Said he left Germany as a kid—" "He left his family?" Rose is suddenly interested. "He looks familiar." "Oh, I don't know. I don't believe—have you heard his accent? He's *German,* and the right age." "But his hair isn't gray," says Stanley. "He doesn't look that old." "Wig," Harry snaps. "Put two and two together. The hero's this U-boat captain by the name of Bauer—his own name's Neu*bauer.* Draw your own conclusions. I told him

'Bauer' didn't sound convincing for the name of a U-boat captain. It should be von-something. 'But zat's his name,' he tells me. Doesn't sound real, I told him, and I believe it. 'You can't even tell if it's man or woman,' I told him. He got offended. 'During ze var,' he said, 'I do not know off any U-boat being commanded by a vooman.' I sure fixed him." "He left his family?" Rose repeats. Mother saunters back and sits down. "Shut up, Harry," she says. There is silence for about a minute. "We have to go," says Rose suddenly. "It's a long drive back." "There's no rush, darling," her spouse ventures. "I told you, they don't close the gates—" "Do stay a little longer," Mother adds, unconvincingly. "Why. Lookee here!" Harry tries to wink at them and smile a welcome to the newcomer at the same time. It twists his face. The lady approaches, smiles, and then veers away to the dessert table. "Did you see that face?" Harry inquires. "Bruises and cuts all over. I asked her yesterday. Fell off my bike, she said. But I've since learned she's had a face-job, and she threw herself off her bike deliberately so as to disguise the bruises and scars." Everybody stands up, except Harry. Rose leans heavily into her crutches. Mother walks ahead. Harry lights up an old stogie, until the manager comes over and points to one of the notices stuck to the wall. He dowses it in a glass of melted ice-water, just as Stanley comes back to retrieve Rose's bag. From the lawn, Rose, Nora and Stanley take in gulls wading in the shallows. "Wyeth colors," says Stanley, who is still holding the bag. Mother glances at him. "Like in *Christine*," he explains. Mother looks again. I follow her gaze. It's true. There is something to what he said. There are light green reeds at the margin, then large rings of brown mud, and then a bled-in yellow. The tidal stream makes big loops before straightening out for the sea. Wooden white gulls are still standing in the shallows. A small man approaches with a German shepherd on a leash of linked steel rings. As he gets nearer, the dog wags his tail. "Lovely dog," says Stanley. "How do you do? Yes! Nice but dumb," says the man. "Dumb? Really? He looks like a very nice dog to me. How come he's dumb?" The man yanks on the leash as the dog tries to lick Stanley's leg. "He's not aggressive," the man says, and hauls the dog off. "We really ought to go," Rose murmurs. "I hate driving in the dark. I see things. Or I'm afraid something will run out and I'll hit it." She hasn't driven for years, since the accident. "I'll drive, dear," says Stanley. "I like night driving. I can concentrate better. There are no distractions. We'll go soon." Harry has caught up with them. "Did you introduce them to the Reverend Whatsisname?" he wheezes. "Hardly," Mother replies. "Was that the man with the dog?" Stanley inquires. "That was no man. That was a sex machine." "Dumped his dog," Stanley notes. "Probably drowned it. Nice animal." "Stanley," Mother pleads, "please don't encourage him!" We all turn to look at the shambling, quick-footed goose-shaped outline of the dog-less Reverend Chapman, now walking with a lady. Above our heads, Canada geese are making their stiff-winged purposeful flight from the salt marshes to the fresh-water pond behind the mansion. The spring-fed pond is home to mallards, colorless, female, mostly. Developers were recently prevented from building over the springs, but water hyacinths thrive on various luxuriant effluents, and are strangling the water. "His wife," Harry whispers. "Oh," says Stanley. "Now I remember. We saw them this morning on your porch just after we arrived. They were facing east, in full prayer-dress, so to speak. They had an open prayer book between them and were singing hymns very quietly. Very spiritual. You remember, dear?" Rose is trying to peek at her watch. "There's a hurricane moving in from the south," she says. "That's them," Harry continues. "Well, the other day, Chris—he cleans the rooms—told me he'd opened their room with his key by mistake. And there was the reverend humping his little old wife. Hump, hump, fizz, fizz / Oh, what a relief it is." He laughs and looks at Mother. "Do you think that man is really a Nazi?" Rose asks. "He is very blond." "Anyways," Harry goes on, "there he is, humping away, and 'Oh, so sorry!' says Chris. And old Chapman, missing hardly a stroke, looks up and says, 'Oh, that's quite all right!' and goes right back on the job. He was still wearing his dog-collar." Harry does a little shuffle step. "Their room's next to mine. He keeps me awake." The sound of a hymn drifts out from the assembly room, accompanied by a slightly off-key piano. The music makes me feel even more invisible than I usually feel on these timeless visits. "We should join the service," Mother suggests. "It's not really a service," says her daughter. "I wish they had real services," Mother muses. "Then I'd go." For a moment we stand and listen.

"Welcome in, take a stand,
as the river of his love turns red
to heal you up again.
Learn the dove's song as she coos it,
we've come too far now to lose it,
but not too far to rechoose it,
Welcome in!"

Amens and alleluias follow. "I once saw him with a copy of *Hustler* inside a newspaper." Harry is nibbling at a nail. "I think *Hustler* degrades women," says Rose. "Right on!" Harry brays, pulling at his thin moustache. "I should think *you're* something in the altogether," he says. "I'd fork out for an issue that spreads *you* across its centerfold." "I think I had a dream somewhat related to that just two nights ago," Stanley interjects, nervously. "There was a huge flash—remember, I told you as we drove here, dear? In the west. Then a physicist tells me they've been having strange reports of what seems to be a pattern of strong storms from the South, but they haven't followed the usual graph-shape—at the end the pattern is broken off, but in a purposeful way." "I've told you," says Rose. "There's a hurricane moving in from the south." "I came looking for you, my dear, because they'd camouflaged their attack as natural phenomena. But when I did find you you told me, 'Go away! I told you I never want to see you again.'"

The strain of another hymn filtered out:

> *"My father, my mother, my daughter, my son,*
> *My sister, my brother, yes, you are the one.*
> *So go share the flavor wherever you are,*
>
> *Give like a lantern and shine like a star.*
> *So don't lose the savor and don't hide the light.*
> *For many are longing and lost in the night.*
> *Amen."*

"I think I'll join them," says Mother. But she only moves a few inches toward the steps. "Which reminds me," Harry muses in a low voice, winking at me, "what *did* happen to your brother?" "We don't talk about him," says Rose. "Ever since that time. To me he's *dead.*" A scraggy procession comes down the wooden steps onto the lawn. Inside, the piano keeps on playing. Voices crack and waver from, for a moment, ageless throats.

> *"I danced on the Sabbath and I cured the lame,*
> *The holy people said it was a shame."*

Mother is about to join in, but instead she looks at me. "Your hair is as white as mine. You used to be so fair. You and your brother, both." She turns to look at Rose. I think I can tell what she's thinking, but when I try I can't. I look at Rose and note that it isn't the aging of the features so much as the falling-in of whatever had held them up. Connect the dots and you come up with nothing. I blink, and look again. For a moment, there is nothing there, just an oval struck out by a slash of light that falls through the maple. It slices through the gap in the foliage a gust of wind has created.

Rose is now sitting in one of the wicker armchairs, her crutches lying parallel beside her like equal signs. Harry has sauntered off. "You never did love me," she says to her mother in her childish voice. "I was always a disappointment to you. You never preferred me. You always gave *him* more than me." Mother lowers herself carefully into the other wicker chair, slowly adjusting her bespectacled eyes to distance, where, in the middle of the salt-marsh a scrub forest has laid down an arm, a streamlined outline. The edge facing the Atlantic lowers progressively; its head goes down and its shoulder humps like a long buffalo. Whatever thoughts she may have had are drowned out by the Reverend Chapman and others singing hymns at the side of the house as if there is no tomorrow: "*So don't lose the savor and don't hide the light, / For many are longing and lost in the night.*" "Stuff!" Mother exclaims. Then, "'No suffering, no cause or end of suffering, no path, no wisdom and no gain.' Does that mean life is futile? That there's no point to it? I feel it means the opposite."

Before I can reply, a shadow falls across her chair. The shadow turns into a wide calico skirt, besprinkled with flowers and small trees. A small torso sits atop wide hips, sinks in, as if dove-tailed. Everything is topped by a face wide, jowly. From under a scarlet bandanna gray hair sticks out. "Anna," Mother says to her daughter, by way of introduction. "I mean, Kristina." "I have to sit," says Rose, by way of explanation. "That's perfectly all right, dear," says Anna/Kristina. Then she says to Mother, "It's Anna, dear. Kristina was who I was in my last incarnation. Now I work through Anna. I don't believe I've seen you here before, have I?" "I come when I can," says Rose. "It's not easy for me." "Nor for any of us, dear," says Anna, bending down to touch the grass. "Still damp." She straightens.

Then, all in one movement, draws her legs up under her and plonks down, to sit like a Buddha. It seems to make Rose uneasy to have this woman's head so close to her elbow. I imagine she is resisting an urge to stick it in her ear. "What do you mean, you work through Anna?" she asks. Anna fishes some hard object from beneath her haunches. "She wishes to channel me," she says. "She wishes to be, let us say, normal." "Channel? Where's she from?" "She tells me she's from Atalanta." "Atlanta?" "No. I'm from Atalanta. I work with entities of the other side." Mother is concentrating on the white steeple across the marsh, rising above the low trees. Then her eyes move left, where a ticky-tacky cottage development had been built, stopping at the water. "The marsh is only here on sufferance," she says to no one in particular. "Nothing has value in itself." "You mean, you work with … *spirits?*" Rose's voice has perked up. "That is very so." "Can you tell the future?" Rose's voice hesitates between hope and doubt. "There is a split coming in Michigan, from Lake Superior down. And man will create earthquakes in the Detroit region because of drugs, murder, and rapes. Look at the city of Detroit. It's malignant!" Mother glances over to Anna, whose face is shining with conviction. "How about Boston?" Rose asks. "I live there. Well, near there." "You are not working on your awareness," Anna replies with some harshness. "You are just sitting back watching television. There will be two years of hard winters." "In Boston?" "There will be a haze over the world." She pauses. "I like you, which is why I am mutually sharing this with you. Would you like me to draw you a spirit guide? You know, I feel we've had a previous encounter." "Well," says Rose, "now I come to think of it, I do sort of remember seeing you last time I came. You know," she lowers her voice, "I'm kind of clairvoyant myself. I *see* things. Did you see that man with blond hair?" "Am I right in feeling you have problems with your colon?" Rose levers herself up.

"Going inside," Mother announces, leaving Anna, Rose and me. Anna moves into Nora's chair. "Tell me about your family." I follow in Mother's wake.

Mother almost bumps into Harry as she walks between the two privet hedges, going into the house by the back way to avoid the people moving into the house before the oncoming storm. Binoculars fall from his hand. "Quite a young lady, that daughter of yours," says Harry, bending to retrieve them. "You were spying on us?" "No. Not you. Her. Quite a full-figured lady. Reminds me of my first wife, may she rest. I like women with—you know. It takes me back to my younger days, when women were women. Here, let me help you." He starts to push back part of the hedge for Mother to pass. "If you'll just step back and out of the way, that would take care of matters nicely, thank you." But Harry persists, and is soon embattled with the hedge like a buck in rut. The bush sways and thrashes about as if a storm is in it. "Oh, get out of the way, you old fool! Talk about galloping ghosts!"

Some large drops of rain are beginning to fall. At the point when Harry has finally extricated himself, there is a yell from the lawn, a yell that rises above the remaining hymn singers and other stragglers. Mother turns her head, notices me, then walks a few steps back to get a better view of what's happening. Through the increasing rain she catches sight of her daughter, both crutches raised, attempting to swat a tall man, who is holding onto his head with one hand, and trying to catch the crutches with the other. "Oh, my God!" Mother whispers. People are now rushing in. Harry tries to push past her. Rose's voice rises in a shriek. "You left us all, when you should have taken care of us, and now you think you can come back whenever you want to!" She swings at him again. Someone shouts for Mrs. Cornell, the chief dietician, to call the police. A jet clamors overhead, adding to the calamity. A crutch comes down on the man's pate, knocking his blondish wig to the grass. He collapses, groaning.

*

Mother is sitting on the litter-strewn porch. I have stayed longer than I intended to help straighten things out. The long ride back to Manhattan will be done in the dark. In the porch light falling onto the lawn I can just make out some birds pecking about the debris. Harry had turned his chair around from the TV within, and is staring at pigeons still moving about under the large low eaves. From time to time, his eyes drop to the piles of black dung on the deck under their nests. "Chicken-wire's broken," he says. "They should repair it. Not supposed to be there. They should be cleared out." "They're doing no harm," Mother replies. "You should go now," she says to me. There is a constant burbling and gargling and cooing, and the feeding of squabs. "I'd better go now," I say. "Breed all year. Never stop. Day and night. On and on. Again and again, never ends," Harry observes. A squab almost falls off the ledge, followed by a great flapping of feathers and much squawking. Feathers cascade down in small storms from time to time. "I think," Mother says, "we should let go of things." "It's better to entertain an idea than take it home to live with you for the rest of your life," I add, trying to impress. "Randall Jarrell," says Harry. I stare at him. Nora turns her head away from the dark marsh to look intently at Harry. "What?" "Randall Jarrell. 'Pictures from an Institution.' Now," he says to me, "my turn. Can you tell me who was known as 'The Galloping Ghost'?" We all turn to look at a noisy plane flying low over the marsh—I push back my chair. I rise.

Not the Real Marilyn Monroe

Ray Wooten of Ochopee is in the process of crowning the latest Miss Swamp Buggy. He takes the opportunity to plug his airboat business to the massed gathering of three or four reporters and, between tobacco squirts, bawls out the feds for being about to take over the Big Cypress Swamp. "Got me bugged too," he snarls. "Trying to bribe me and them other holdouts with parking concessions in the swamp. Who wants to *park* in a swamp?"

Meanwhile, in Coral Gates, his great-aunt Ethel May Burdick, 81, and her friend Maribel Budd, 88, are enjoying a belated Thanksgiving dinner at the Riviera Country Club. Suddenly, a cherry jubilee dessert explodes and sets their clothing on fire. Ethel will be admitted to Jackson Memorial Hospital and detained, but Maribel will be treated and released.

And all the while this is going on, Ray Wooten will be trying to offer Miss Swamp Buggy a ride over the Big Cypress Swamp in one of his airboats. It goes without saying that his attempts will be received with modesty and half-open ears. For Miss Swamp Buggy is stuck on one Jonathan, a grad student at the University of Florida, who, at the very moment when Miss Swamp Buggy finally relents and takes off, will be chewing on a quote from a book he is reading in the library: "Behold, I show you a mystery: we shall not all sleep, but we shall all be changed."

*

119

But as you saw, Ray is no slouch. He sees a weakness and goes for you, smooth as a gator entering water. Now I'm the generous sort, and my mother's a great cook, which is why Ray ended up at our place. And I wasn't exactly surprised when he put his penis in one of the plastic mugs my mother had set on the table. He realized he had forgotten to fill it. So he extracted his organ, set the mug under the tap, turned on the water, and waited. When the mug was full of lukewarm liquid he again set it under his penis and began washing. When he had finished, he walked over to the dishtowel rack and wiped himself dry. Nice touch. My mother was not pleased. "What's going on? I leave you in charge and you end up allowing some jerk to wipe his dick on my teatowel." "But first he washed it in the plastic mug—" "Out!" my mother called. Ray took it all in his stride. Pocketing a hush puppy, he left with a wink in my direction. My mother spun round to me. "Every time I turn on the oven the fridge defrosts. And now *this!*" "He couldn't understand our ways," I said. "He's rural." "We'll forget it for the present. Go and make the tea. And turn off the oven. And wipe up the water from the floor."

The kettle was puffing out steam like a locomotive. Through the door opposite I could see Mr. Richard at a long table, going through a pile of suggestions for coordinating those humanitarian drives the organization specialized in. "We need more political prisoners," he remarked to his delightful young assistant, who wasn't very interested, but who was very sincere. "We're running out of causes to champion." "There do seem to be less each year," she replied vaguely, as if she was talking of Indian lions, mountain gorillas, or blue whales. "Perhaps a new wave of repression will sweep the world."

I walked in with my teapot, all wrapped in its hand-crocheted cozy. I'd forgotten the cups and milk and sugar, as well as the spoons. I hoped nobody would notice. I looked over the girl's shoulder as she was sorting these members who had paid their dues from those who had not. I had not. "Here," I said helpfully, "let me do that for you while you pour the tea." "Into what?" she inquired, pert. I ignored her, and handed her the teapot so fast she had no alternative but to grab it. "Well," she said, and went off for the necessaries.

While she was gone I falsified the books. To my surprise, I saw that not only had I not paid up for last year, but I hadn't fulfilled my obligations for the last five years. Yet I still received mail and invitations—not that I wouldn't have gone anyway, since I lived at HQ. To make bookkeeping easier for all concerned, I noted in my best rapid handwriting that I had paid my dues regularly on time. I also wrote that I had paid up for another five years in advance. The postage saved organizations would be enormous if committees required everyone to do what I had just done. It would save all sorts of follow-up letters to follow-up letters, etc. "What happened to that man and his penis?" my mother called in wooly tones from the kitchen, where she had just taken out her teeth. The girl was returning with a tray of jingling things. "Seems he found the atmosphere here oppressive and not conducive to the free flow of ideas," I replied, making it all up as I went along. "The point is," said Richard (*Mr.* Richard), "that we haven't had an increase in membership for thirty years." "Maybe we could count that man and his penis as two," the girl suggested. "Three, more like," said my mother. Then, after a pause, "or maybe even four."

*

When I moved out of my mother's place, I got my own apartment. Mrs. Brown, large and black, cleaned my apartment for the first six months. She wouldn't touch a drop of liquor, even at Christmas, but made no bones about asking me for a cash present and intimidating me into regular raises for her irregular cleaning. When she went to visit her husband and other four children in Trinidad, she announced she was sending her daughter in her place, and got me to agree to an hourly rate of eight dollars. I retaliated by asking the girl, on her first visit, to come every other week instead of each week. She worked fast, but not always accurately. She managed to miss the tops of things and left brushes and vacuum cleaner parts strewn when she left. I didn't complain and we got along well. She always asked for permission to turn on rock music. I acceded, closing the study door, continuing with my work.

Our formal relationship became less formal, and we'd chat about her desire to become a nurse. She graduated from high school the first year she cleaned for me, and in the second began college. By this time, she didn't want to be a nurse, but preferred a career as a veterinarian or doctor. Her name was Margaret. She would eat lunch when she arrived on Saturdays, bringing yogurt or an apple, eating as she worked. When she used the toilet she'd flush as soon as she went in so I wouldn't hear her splashing. If I made anything—soup, bread or whatever—I'd always ask her to try it. We sometimes discussed language, since I finished college. She was starting Swahili, and brought her notebook for me to look at. "Why Swahili?" I asked. "I tried Spanish last year," she replied, "but got hung up over the grammar." I reminded her that from the look of the book, Swahili had a grammar too. "Hadn't thought of that," she said.

One day she arrived late. "Sorry," she gasped. "I just left my boyfriend." "Left him for what?" "What?" "Nothing." "I'm starved!" She dove into a brown sack and brought out some plain yogurt. "Here, mix it with some honey?" Not enthused about my health-food habits, she reluctantly dipped her spoon in the hardened gold. "We dissected a pig today." I was flipping through the pages of Vesalius. "Did you eat it?" "Silly! Not that kind. A small pig. A fetus. It was very interesting. You can see what you're like—kidneys and lungs and things. And did you know its penis went straight into its bladder?" "Where else would it go?"

(At this stage, I should, perhaps, say that I am a white Caucasian male, 5'7" to 5'10", fair-haired—or I could be wearing a wig. I call myself by the name everyone had come to know me by. I was not unknown. One night I watched a Florida State Classics Professor demonstrate on TV, with the use of a blackboard and chalk, that, spelled backward, a name very like mine in Greek meant "mass murderer.")

And it did so happen that one day a woman was murdered in my small apartment. I picked up the phone to call for the emergency number I'd forgotten. But no one answered. I tried again later after I'd found the number in the fridge's ice-tray when I went to get the house keys. I dialed and asked for the police. When I got through, a desk sergeant answered. "We have a priority system, you know. That's why you couldn't get through. We stack up calls and give priority to crimes still in progress, in the hope of apprehending the actual perpetrators at the particular time of the alleged offense." I hung up.

Margaret walked in. I noticed a pimple on her left cheek. "I see you've had a facelift," I said. She denied it. "A woman's been murdered here," I told her. "I don't see nobody," she remarked after a quick look round. "Perhaps you did it. Or them rotten birds." "That's no way to refer to Paula and Rudy. And look, the door's open. You just walked in. Anybody could have walked in. A friend of mine was here just a while ago. He could have done it." "Still don't see no body," she persisted, irritating female. I took her by the arm into the middle room, the bedroom. "There," I said. "A streak of blood, and a little pool." "I don't see anything," she said. "You made it all up."

I got angry at her, and accidentally knocked onto the floor a white china teacup with a silver rim which my old landlady had given me as a going-away present, and which I treasured. It burst like an electric bulb. I stared at the shards in amazement. It was time to get married again. Or move away. "Why is your liquor cabinet always open?" Margaret asked. "There's a broken bottle on the floor and I ain't cleaning up the mess. Them birds enough."

*

I was dreaming my wife had married a small plump man in a brown velvet suit that continued up over his head. Then I was awake. I sat up, forehead cold and damp. My hand moved to the old emptiness at my side. Something in my sleep I had called "The Plot of the Mice" ... I forced my eyes wide. The first thing they became conscious of was the rocking chair. And where she had left them, the koala in the arms of his mother, both snugly encircled by Stanley the cobra. My wife used to send messages this way.

I almost fell out of bed. On cold tiles I dipped and danced to the bathroom, the cold sending little shocks to my brain. I peed, counting off the seconds. 55. Almost a record. I crossed the room to wash my face. Eyes shut and wet, I reached for the soap. Fingers closed round something that felt like an arrowhead. I pulled back my hand as if stung. The Ivory, new the day before, had been nibbled down to an expert Clovis blade. I dried, slumped into the kitchen. Was about to fill the kettle, when I felt something rattling about inside. I pulled off the top. Mouse shit, plump black grains. Disgusted, I held the kettle upside down over the sink. I scoured the inside with Brillo and Ajax. My mind opened. How the hell did the mice get in? They couldn't have squeezed down the spout. And if they did, how did they get out?

The water boiled. As I poured it over my Nestlé's chocolate, I blotted out what might still be in the water. Chocolate contains the same hormones as those secreted when you're in love. I'd read that. I added another heaping spoonful. I stirred the cup, then set it aside. How could I drink chocolate at such a time? I stood up.

Panties still hung from the kitchen doorknob. I let them hang: a scented gift and remembrancer, the flag of my disposition, out of hopeful green stuff woven, bearing the owner's name someway in the corner.

I slouched into the living room and sat down with O. Henry's *Best*. Ah, Woody Allen. That's better. Deep, deep. The man is a genius. Who else could play on one string and for so long and without pausing for a break? Such *plots!* You need a plot to grow things in, otherwise they just turn wild and scatter all over the place, haywire. I began to feel better, if only for the fact of plot … jars, bags, pots, pockets. *Ordnung!* Sometimes, I thought, plots have to be worked for. Sometimes they must just seem to arrive. Maybe they have a life of their own. My hand wandered to my wife's two-month old *Monthly Labor Review*. More plots! "Spendable earnings: have they outlived their usefulness?" Before I could answer, my wrist exploded in beeps. I tore off my Casio Alarm Chronograph, which I hadn't remembered putting on. Then I bent and picked it up gently, like a small animal. I linked it up again. Lists, numbers, graphs. Love means gross weakly yearnings. Ha ha. I found myself staring at Milton Friedman, my wife's favorite economist. I snapped on the radio.

Some friends from Mineola, friends since childhood, on their way back from a party, had swerved round a crossing gate into the path of an oncoming train. A priest was eulogizing them. He recalled how, at their high school graduation, the youth who had driven the van had given the thumbs-up sign to his parents, "as if to say, 'We made it.' And now I imagine him giving the thumbs-up sign to St. Peter, as if to say, 'We made it.'" I snapped off the radio.

And stopped in my tracks. Suddenly, everything seemed clear, significant, formed. A phrase of my mother's drifted into my mind from years before: "All right, children, today we will have Polite Singing." And my father, faithful unto death to the Trade Union Unity League, arms like lianas, drifted in too, saying in radio tones, "Protectionism never worked. Look at the thirties when the system collapsed. 'Beggar Thy Neighbor.' Raise import taxes, abolish export restraints!" I walked about, strangely excited. Total osmosis. No more semi-permeable membranes. Let it all pass through! No more plots! I dropped back onto the sofa. Counted my pulse against the Casio Alarm Chronograph. 130. Almost a record.

I staggered back to bed. Without being aware that I had crawled into my wife's side, I slipped between the sheets. I felt as if I was lying down on an icecap. I stiffened. Something cold against my sole. Metal. A lump. I moved my foot slowly. And shart irritating nodules. My hand crept down. I threw off the covers. A kitchen knife. Dried mouse shit. And, in little heaps, seeds—grass seed, sunflower seed, all sorts of seeds.

*

Janice decided that the purest response to her vision was complete silence, plus apathia and aphasia. After my first divorce, not only did she refuse my offer of a life of bliss together, but she began to make arrangements to submerge herself in a water-filled box where she planned, like a Sioux on a remote mountain-top, to demand a final revelatory vision to direct her life, or else perish in the attempt. I respected her integrity, but never went to visit her again. She had an older sister named Doreen, whom I'd met a couple of times, and liked. So I made a date. I looked forward to that date all month, and planned to stay the whole weekend in the city. Somewhat shaken by a trainride that resembled an Atlantic crossing in a rowboat, I took a cab from Grand Central. I amused myself, and calmed my stomach, by reading various stickers on cars and walls on the way down to the Village. STAMP OUT RAPE: SAY YES. WOMANS MOVEMENT: IT FEELS GOOD. AMERICAN GUN ASSOCIATION. TREE POWER. I soon bored of this, but my attention perked when a truck went by with FIORDELLA FLORAL SYSTEMS INC EXTERIOR AND INTERIOR. Yet it all seemed so ephemeral. I, on the other hand, was about to spend an eternal weekend.

I stopped the cab a few blocks from the apartment in order to light a cigarette, walk a bit to calm down, and enter nonchalently, as if I'd stopped by as an afterthought. I'd hardly reached my destination when I saw thick oilsmoke pouring from vents. I put out my cigarette, in case the fumes were inflammable, and pushed past a line of people descending the staircase with buckets of glowing coals. Was each one getting a piece of the action?

Whatever it was, I reached Doreen's open door and walked in. A fire glowed in the grate. Doreen raised her high Irish eyebrows in answer to my raised shoulders. An old woman stood by the fire with an impatient empty bucket. Doreen went to the fridge and, returning, thrust a Bud into my hand. "Be with you in a minute," she said. Then she walked back over to the hearth where she began doling our needfire like an ancient goddess. I went over to the bedroom and discovered that it lacked a bed. I looked at myself in the mirror. But before I could appreciate myself fully, my attention was diverted by the arrival in the living-room of a little man with a built-up boot. Close behind was a middle-aged woman with built-up hair, shiny as a lacquered doorknob. "They haven't come because you haven't given them any under-table money," the woman yelled, in a tone that made her sound as if she'd been saying the same thing without interruption throughout all the cold days she'd suffered. Doreen ignored her, but when she continued beyond all patience, she grabbed the woman by the shoulders and hustled her out of the room. She turned to the man with the built-up boot. "Coke? Snow? Cash? You name it. It's yours." "Nothin'," said the little man. "You can have anything. Name it." "You." "Don't get fresh." "I shouldn't be doin' this. I shouldn't be here. If they find out … You got me here by a trick." "Grass?" She seemed to know him well. He said nothing. Turning, he bent and picked up some tools. Unlocking the door, he left. Soon the billows of smoke that had been swirling around the window ceased.

Doreen had walked over to the fridge. She unscrewed the top of a screw-top beer. "What happened?" "Oh, nothing," she replied, taking a swig. "I was out of town for a week, I told you. Left a friend in charge—I've been super for three weeks. When I go back yesterday I found he'd skipped off, and so had some of my furniture. I found the tenants ready to lynch me. Seems soon after I left the heat went off, so they made him go down to the basement to see why there'd been no heat. He saw there was no fuel. But what he didn't see was that the ignition had blown. So when he threw the switch—boom!" "So why didn't he call the repairman?" "Why? Because they've been on strike all month, right?" There was a banging at the door. Doreen opened it, and there were three or four huge buckets attached to three or four arms. "Help yourself," Doreen told them. "We're going out."

When we got back from all sorts of errands it was about bedtime. Except there was no bed. Doreen dragged two crumpled rubber skins out of a closet, and we proceeded to inflate them. All night, her ten Maine Coon cats bounced

128

up and down on us bouncing up and down on the life-rafts. By morning I was ready to retreat to the suburbs. But before catching the 12:05 back to Norwalk, I made the mistake of wandering around the Village. In Washington Square Park I sat down by the dustbowl of a fountain. A visitation materialized in the form of a 4'1" brunette. "Eighteen months ago," she intoned, "I was like so many other women. So I decided to diet. My intention was to reduce my 'nicely distributed' 128-pound frame to about 111 pounds. The diet succeeded. I conceded I was happy at my new weight of 103 pounds. But I was not happy enough." "Excuse me," I said, getting up carefully so as to avoid a mountainous black man on roller skates, whose entire being was involved with the huge earphones clamped to his head. He was moaning and singing to accompany his disco twists and slides. In avoiding his wheels, however, I stumbled into an older man who had probably been playing chess in the quiet southern corner of the park. "I'm sorry," he said. "I'm sorry too," I replied. "But probably not as sorry as I," he insisted. "We have to exist in a world that shuns and avoids definition, and so we stick with a conception of reality that rests upon a fluidity of presentation. Like that young man on wheels." I nodded, trying to sidestep him. He threw a neat block. "You understand competition? Right. Unfair, right? We have to be able to respond and react, but every time we innovate we find outselves actually following." I nodded again, and again tried to push past him. But this time my escape route was blocked by another roller-skater whose back, I saw as he turned round, was covered by a sign that said ROLLER FAIRY. The sun glinted on the small dainty pair of silver wings that sprang from his shoulderblades. My eyes dropped to his hairy legs, decorated at the ankle with an even daintier pair of silver wings. I turned, and tried the other side. There was the 103-pound lady. "It's the nature of the modern world," the old man continued.

"Symbolized by that blasted supermarket across the street from me." "Ah, San Marco, San Giorgio, the Doge's Palace!" I spun round. "My wife," the old man explained. "Oh," I said, eyeing the violin case she toted. "What I came for," said the anorexic young woman, "is for some hot dogs from the guy on the corner over there. I am obsessed by food. I will prepare entire meals for my family, even bake for my friends, but never consume what I prepare." "Mm," said the wife, fumbling with the catch on the case. "Starvation seems to be your ultimate goal. You wish to gain complete control of your biological, physiological, and emotional reasons to exist. Over-control means death. You have to allow chance into your life to put flesh on your bones." Her husband interrupted. "The real reason has to do with how you feel about yourself." A strange voice emanated from behind me. I spun round. There was the Roller Fairy, headphones off. "Did you read about the two elderly women who were burned when their holiday dessert exploded?" he asked the old man. But before he could hear the answer, he was pushed to the ground by two other black men, and sat on, his wheels spinning. "Just lie there, man. Lie back," one of the men ordered. "I ain't got no clothes, and I ain't got no food. I'm a real sonofabitch, man. And you can't lay all that bad smack on me, man." The Roller Fairy lay quiet. Then, seeing his chance, he leapt to his wheels, and was soon hightailing it out of the park, the other two weaving, chasing, and cursing. I got up and walked over to the fountain where, in its dry bowl, a tall bald man was delivering monologues like in London's Hyde Park. He had just finished one that seemed to be in the voice of Marilyn Monroe and was beginning another with a British accent: "I am Cecil Beaton. I am not Katherine Hepburn, that raddled piece of decayed matter. I am not the Queen Mum, that pink cushiony cloud, nor her daughter, who tapped me on each shoulder in '77 and said 'Rise.' I am not Bianca Jagger, nor Lady Diane Cooper, Collette, the other Hepburn, or any of the rest, though I took up much of Garbo's 'vuarghluobbhle' time and tedious personality propped on her pillows, and would have married her under the Third Avenue L despite my prostate and hormone treatments that shrank my penis and swelled my breasts so I could no longer squeeze myself into a size too small. But I am still Cecil Beaton, still persona grata here among my innumerable portraits and my hundred and forty-five notebooks as I watch the Queen Mum discreetly watching other diners to see which fork she should use for lobster. Yes, I am still Cecil Beaton here in the realm of Pluto—" he looked about, waved his arms to encompasses us all, "giver of wealth, clicking my shutters—" he clicked imaginary shutters, "as the famous and rich stretch out at ease on this lovely greensward, waiting for me to make them and tell them who they are." "We should view all this from a global perspective," murmured the old man. Then he turned to me with a look of great sincerity. "Can you spare an old man 100 dollars to get home to Brooklyn?" Out of the corner of my eye I saw his wife finally free the catch on her violin case. Clamping my hand over my heart, I backed off. Then ran through the graffitied Arch of Triumph. In my mind they were all after me. I thought about sprinting. I began to sprint. I sprinted all the way up 5th Avenue, dodging bicycles going the wrong way against the traffic, and ignoring traffic lights myself.

*

From my office I can see the center of the world. I spend more time watching outside than feeding my computer. The window is squared off like one of Dürer's grids. People move from one rectangle to the other. They are inevitable. Given a certain shape, people can only act relentlessly. Cars line the sidewalk, heads in, pastel popcorn teeth. They too have been there always.

Only the shadows from high-rise and co-op move, closing over the cars, moving them. Voilá! Today's special. A woman climbs in the baby carriage with the baby. A father, tired of fielding, clubs his son with the bat.

Furniture sits on the sidewalk as if the room around it had suddenly melted away. The sky drifts. As for me, the night before I had dreamed of an eagle squeezed inside a telescope. Flattening the whole thing under a page, I wrote the number 10 on it. When I opened the page, the eagle began to push out the telescope.

In the office next door, my secretary is bent over her loins inhaling the odor like the priestess at Cumae.

The blank page in the typewriter holds her prophecies.

*

On the way home I stop in a small shop. "Balkan Sobranie, please." "How's your cat? What your cat?" He goes up the ladder to small refrigerator. "The cat. When is she? Black or white?" "Gray ... oh, I—black." He sorts out change. "Seventy-five. Two." "The—OK. Thanks."

I almost have to push by the two streetwalkers. One, like the women I used to see outside the Weyerhauser plant in Longview, WA, where the old lady took me at age ten to visit her sister, after my father ran off. Old West look, hair drawn back off forehead, and a face staring out, not seeming to listen to her black friend, whose strong legs divide at about my elbow. Face like a snapping turtle. "Right, then. I'll call you. Later."

A pigeon lands on the curb, folds his wings. Jumps with both feet together into the gutter, like a child jumping into a pond. It reminds me of the drawing done by a child, "terminally ill," who'd been asked to draw what death meant to him. First he drew a plank over a lake with him standing on it. Then he just drew the plank.

I turn up 2nd Avenue off 14th Street. Hard to believe that there was a spring here when Manhattan was covered by forest and Indian tracks. A U-Haul truck backs into a tree. The street people and bag ladies are out in force. It is the first day of spring. I have forgotten to put my watch forward. I recognize one woman from a TV documentary. She slides along a walk, two plastic bags like floats. Pulling her arms down. A young woman, from the Caribbean, still some Carib in her. Her eyes slide left to me, rabbit eyes. She looks as if she is about to cry. I recall I'd heard her say yes, she was frightened. No, she had no friends. Yes, lonely. No, she was not the real Marilyn Monroe.

*

In such a world I turned to social diversions. Parties. One after another, so they became a blur. But two still stick in my mind.

At the party I gave to celebrate Paula's birthday, a rather startling event took place. Willard, scholar and translator author of nineteen books and a man of serious deportment suddenly broke into song. We were so taken aback that we all joined in. Harmonies became the order of the day, each person naturally taking a part, like the customers in an Elizabethan barber shop, or the crowd at a Welsh rugby game.

"You know," said Willard breaking off midway through a lesser-known lieder of Sklert, at the start of which we had lost him, "you know, I'm proficient in fifty-two languages. One for each week of the year. I'm at the point where I know a language in all its dead forms as well as its living dialects—I'm not counting those dialects in the total. I even know Bushman, classic Kalahari form." "Fascinating," said Penelope, breaking open an orange. "Say some." "I shall," Willard snapped pushing an embroidered pillow away from the back of his head. He stood up. "*Tsk tsk tsk tsk tsk tsk.*" "What's *that?*" (a female voice). "*That* is the verb 'to be.'" "But it's all the same," said the same voice, simultaneously surprised and disappointed. "Well now, yes," Willard conceded. "Now you come to mention it, yes, I suppose it is." "Perhaps it says something about their world vision," Maud piped in. She had just graduated from Sarah Lawrence. "Or perhaps their sense of self is not yet distinguished from the totality of their environment." That from her brother Sean, who had a terrible singing voice and didn't even try to improve it. "Like singing," said a rather clammy voice from the floor at the end of the sofa. "Singing is all notes and is undifferentiated within the context it sets up for itself. The parts are only distinguished by pitch, duration, and quality. May I ask if you learned that verb from a book of actual field-trip observation?" "A book," Willard frowned. "I learn all my languages from books. Do you think I can afford the time to dash off to all corners of the earth every time the desire strikes me to add another language to my collection?" "Well," replied the voice, now possessed by someone I had never seen before, and I'm sure had never invited to the party, a beetle-browed youth with a hat still on, and beads, someone I'm sure Paula would never approve of, "well, isn't it likely that the Bushman language is a music of differentiations; a music of few symbols but an enormous number of tonal colors and variations? You could only get their meaning by hearing, not from reading."

Silence dropped like a tree on somebody's roof. Willard's face became a mask of scholarly fury. But before any altercation could get going, someone said, "Let's all sing 'The Lark In the Clean Air.'" "*Clear* air!" screamed Willard. And thus the situation was defused. But the noise was so violent, in fact, that I feared for the sanity of Paula and Rudy. I went into the basement and lifted Paula from her pile of woodshavings, stuffing her safely into the breastpocket of my vest, where her badtempered squirmings were, I must say, a little discomforting. Then I went to Rudy in the bedroom, disregarding his large mandibles, for he too was ill-tempered at having been woken. I managed to get him inside my shirt where I soon got used to his scratching and tearing. I looked about carefully for a quiet spot to deposit them both, out of harm's way, and I must have made quite a spectacle of myself, scooting around, probing under beds, into wardrobes, under dresses. My task wasn't made any easier by the fact that Paula and Rudy kept escaping, darting straight at the ceiling, where they received some nasty knocks. Eventually Paula disappeared down the back of the Castro convertible which was in the process of being pulled out so that a warm discussion between Willard and June Brugg could be conducted with a great deal more comfort. Needless to say, Paula was crushed in the process, and although everybody concerned apologised, it was really nobody's fault. Poor Paula. On her birthday too. And if that wasn't enough, I discovered that Rudy must have been sick for some time without my noticing (probably an imbalance of the inner ear), for on one of his dives on somebody's head he misjudged both distance and velocity and made an awful, not to say fatal, landing. I suppose the noise and confusion of the party were just too much for them, poor dears.

It was a nice party, but a sad one.

*

I put on the TV without the sound and watched them battle for silent points. It was the movement I needed. The night before, a rat had come in the open window and woken me with its heavy feet. Then I turned off the TV, went and got some ratbane and, rather against my conscience, put some through the hole in the ceiling. I walked into the kitchen, looked through the fridge, nibbled and sipped. It has become a habit. I even ate white bread I hated and drank ketchup right from the bottle. I poured party-sprinkles into the palm of my hand and swallowed them. Then I carefully arranged everything the way it had been and went to bed.

OLD NEW YORK

*The progress of literature seems to me to consist in the gradual
removal of unnecessary fictions ... the story becomes superfluous,
what matters more is the communication of experiences, linguistic
and non-linguistic ones.*
——Peter Handke

Tom Garvey, a gray-haired biker, the original Happenings, I
was there, Tosün's buckets of pig blood on the Bowery in the
'60s, he became a Whirling Dervish, "Inside Out," the usual
roster, teeming meditation on surveillance, BAM's Morris'
zany take on "The Fairy's Kiss," it takes 35 gallons of water to
make a cup of coffee, like a spring breeze, the "architecture of
Loss," including risk and loss like ballet and Fidelity Brokerage
Services, the best kind of cultural ambush, ambassadors who
see opportunity in white plastic armchairs or Luigi Ghirr's
"Nogara 1989" or Beethoven's "Missa Solemnis" at the Met, a
vibrant modernist ensemble suffusing the park's erotic trance,
an ardent clap, turn here to Fidelity Investments, a script
by Tom Shepard in Nazi-occupied Lvov, savor the journey
in Ozone Park, Sung-Nam's cavalier behavior toward her,
revivals, classics, etc., a prog-rock pioneer, A-list producer,
through March 18, "Kotoka," through March 10, in Japanese,
through 1988, Clause Souter, in French, Enid Starkie eating
lunch beside Marvin Cohen's bathtub full of dirty dishes, the
free-wheeling pursuit of experience, "Fuck you, if you want
to be French," happiness too, Dubai on Green Street, lemon
in the calamari, "the egg is a musky pleasure," Gael too, "Fix

'er up, chef!", strawberries in her organ loft, hacked chicken at Hunan, "a poet friend haunted by violence," called me "*mon bite,*" if you want to be French, Waste Makes Haste, the Yorkville *Nutcracker,* gale of laughter, a society born on the edge of violence, alluring deception and suave surfaces, ping-pong witticisms, sitting next to Piper Laurie at dinner, not a word, Martha Schlamme my hostess, in wide release, March 2-3, Signature Dance Company, Tatiana lost her handbag in the subway, *The Red Shoes,* Massine, Coline C., hardly more than a girl, whose initialed panties I still keep as scented remembrancer, "The signature of all things" I am here to read, Judy Beck, *Playboy* centerfold, whose girlfriend had two vaginas, Stephen Bosch, midsummer night's city as orgasm, "a mark upon any matter, particularly upon plants," planted evidence in the park, Shakespeare in the Park, dinner with Peter and Tom, Tompkins and Kuhn, the secret life of structure, erasure and cancellation, I was there.

YOU'RE IT

Her twin sister penetrates women so deep they vomit. Sometimes they make out. "It's hard to tell where one ends and the other begins." Her present lover has two vaginas and is the only woman she knows who has a better body. They took mushrooms. She had a vision of making love to herself and giving birth in a mirror she couldn't get out of. "The mirror made me pregnant." She's "into everything." Everything she wears she stole. She reaches into her deep bag, holds up a *Playboy* centerfold. "Do you want to see? Yes, Miss May, 1970, it's me. Don't touch! This always happens. Last week at an orgy twelve men and two women jumped on me. Horrible. And on a trip to Haifa I was raped by a very virile guy who kept coming. 'Look,' I said, 'do what you want but let me get up.' 'I'll go get a whore,' he said." She puts the photo back in the bag. "In college I was a topless dancer. What those men would have given for just one night with me. I played them like fish." She's "androgent," but won't accept anything under ten inches. "One needed so much blood to fill, he fainted." Men are fools but women are a threat. "I want to penetrate and impregnate. I want to be a desirable woman." At a bar in the Village a woman she didn't know said, "*Miriam, the spirit of your mother wants you to return to your roots.*" "I burst out crying. My mother died when I was twelve. Now I'm twenty. What will happen to me? Will anyone remember me?" She goes into her bag. "Open your mouth." I do, and she blows a New Year party blowout into it. "Now you're it," she says.

WOMEN IN SHAKESPEARE

Manicured hands catch at something floating in the air. "You use the sugar-tongs thusly." She was once a Hare Krishna, then a Jehovah's Witness, Mother says. Now she keeps her past for its parts. Reclining on her antimacassar, Cleopatra on her burnished barge, she sets aside her tinkling teacup, and rises to shake crumbs from her kimono. She takes a few steps, as if to practice, carrying herself like a precious cargo. "Look around you." Old playbills. "Art is more than a cry. I hate sloppy emotion. I would rather drink mandragora. Art is meant to save and heal, don't you agree, darling? We all need to heal. Nobody is ever what they were. It's like being posted somewhere else. We all need a new place to stand and evaluate our lives, past, present, and to come. I don't suppose you've heard of Theosophy, have you, dear?" The voice of Phèdre kicks in. "I can't stand heavy people. What do they call them now?" "Heavy-boned." She sighs, languid as a tall building. "Don't play with the doilies, darling. Their skin is like tissue paper. It can split and spill them all over. Do you know there are no fat women in Shakespeare? No—one lump at a time, like this, firm but gentle. Otherwise they shoot all over the place and it's the very devil to get down and fish them out from under things— well, if you don't mind you'll have to leave soon. I'm visiting the Lillian Booth, (they have a small theater, *trés intime*), with my *Women in Shakespeare*. One mustn't lose track of who one is, don't you think? I see you looking at the playbill, *Cigarettes and Cake*. We almost made the West End, but anything to do with cigarettes these days, or cake, is the kiss of death. Well, I must get ready. Darling, can you open the window, it's rather close in here. Ah, for this relief, much thanks. And so, farewell. Please leave the tongs. Everyone should have tongs, don't you think? But they should buy their own. Goodbye, sweet thing, my poet. I do so love poetry. And how's the family? Do come again. Oh, a poem before you go. Something classic." "OK," I say. "*Ich ver alt, ich ver alt, und min pupik vert mir kalt.*" "Rilke?" she asks. "Heine," I say.

SPENDING THE NIGHT

He refused to exchange the ticket for her. That's all she did. Buy and exchange. Or she bought and he exchanged. She'd drawn him in with store credits. No money changed hands. He was bad with money. But then false names and addresses, crazy phone numbers were added to the mix. When he was required to fill in a replacement credit slip after a purchase where there was change, he'd panic and write his real name and address, and real phone number. This led to spats on his return home, and accusations of incompetence. False names, addresses and phone numbers were scattered all over the city. They piled up. None of it made sense to him. Then one day he put his foot down. He would not exchange the ticket for her. Nor would he back down, as he usually did.

That evening, he was walking near the old Yiddish theater, now the "Orpheum," on 2nd Avenue. He stopped. He would not go home. Ever. As he mused, he was almost hit by a bicycle on the sidewalk. What next? He thought. A grown woman on a bicycle, what next? He leaned against the wall and remembered reading how we come out of the womb a month early, looking like a fetal chimpanzee. If we'd stayed the correct time we wouldn't have our flat faces, high foreheads, hairless bodies and big toes completely useless for grasping and holding. So we stay immature. We never grow up. Perpetual children in looks and bodies and minds. And there was that middle-aged woman pedaling along the sidewalk on a toy, capable of doing great damage. He looked about. Twenty-somethings on skateboards popping up and down in gutters, thirty-somethings buzzing along against the traffic on shiny aluminum scooters. He wandered off until, looking about, he realized he was outside Maurice's apartment building on Lafayette, near the American Indian Community Center. Maurice was Mohawk though, as they say, he didn't look Indian. He punched in the bell code and waited. A disembodied voice demanded his identity. Maurice had a small apartment, full of old furniture, heavy, dark, mostly oak. All the chairs were occupied. Maurice, a neat, compact man, was having one of his many parties. "Let's eat," he announced. Friends sat at table and other friends served. Huge platters, steaming hot, and on each a whole fish surrounded by piles of boiled potatoes and something that looked like cabbage. Everybody was happy. But he couldn't eat. Nor could he ask Maurice to let him stay there. Apart from anything else, there was no room. So he left, and after walking around for a while he decided to try Art who lived on Spring. When he got there he squeezed by children playing in the corridors and started to climb, the noise from above him getting louder. He thought Art lived on the top floor and climbed a couple of floors until he came to two men's shirts tied together at the sleeves and stretched across the stairs. A hand-made sign said not to pass that point. He pressed on, temporarily entangling himself and ignoring a woman who paused amid pails and mops to stare at him. He asked if she knew where Art's apartment was. She pointed upward.

At the very end of the very top floor, at the end of a long corridor, a door stood open. The room was well lit, and though he couldn't see Art he knew he was there. He slipped in. A discussion was in progress. He tried to get the gist, but couldn't. He didn't know anybody. Then, "We've been looking for you everywhere," said a voice. It was Art, a man about his own age. They both sat down on the floor. A young woman joined them and took Art's hand. "Go and stay with June," Art said. "She likes you. You can stay as long as you like." "I, I don't know her," he said. The girl smiled, got up, and left. "Let's go for a walk," said Art. "It's noisy in here."

They walked down the stairs and out onto the street. Art was happily married, but rumor said he was living with another woman at the same time. He had a gray moustache and gray hair, balding. He also had a little paunch and was a wine connoisseur. They walked a block, saying little, until they reached an apartment building and knocked on a door with a Slavic name on it.

"Genna will be glad to see you," Art said. "We've made dinner." "I thought you said her name was June." The door opened and a lovely young blonde greeted them. "Of course you can stay," she said. He looked from one to the other. "No," he said. "I'd better go."

The night was chilly now, early fall. An unnatural light came off streetlights. Where would he spend the night? Or other nights. He felt in his pockets. Nothing. Not well thought out. He looked up at all the lighted windows. Traffic and voices, hurry scurry. He passed a hotdog vendor talking in broken English to customers. Where would he spend the night. "Spend," he thought. What a strange idea. Who would buy the night. Who would want it? What would he get in exchange?

Ring of Fire

"If you think everything stays the same as it always was, then you've got another think coming," said the person who lives in my hair. "I've lost the key, I've lost the key, again," said my father, turning everything upside down while my mother looked on calmly. "What's new?" she said. "At least this time you haven't lost the car." I looked out the window to the driveway. "No car," I said. "Comb your hair, Sam," my mother said. "It's a rat's-nest." "Maybe it's in the street," my father said, dashing out, and dashing back a few minutes later. "It's nowhere. I can't find it anywhere. I can't remember where I left it." "Don't you own a comb? When are you going to get it cut?" my mother said. "Never," I replied. "And what's a comb got to do with anything?" "Did I tell you where I left it?" my accountant father asked, foraging in the well-stocked liquor cabinet. "You did not," she said. "It'll turn up. It always does. Always the same." "Not always," I said. "But what's the use of a car without the key?"—my father from under the sofa. "It's not here. I put it somewhere safe. It'll turn up. It always does." "Not always," I said. "Lost and found, found and lost, I don't know how we go on. You don't see me losing things," said my mother, a Buddhist who believed in reincarnation. "You lost me as a baby," I said. My father emerged from under the sofa with a silver hip flask and a dream-catcher. "It's a jungle under there," he muttered. "Dust, dust mice, mice." "Don't hurt them," said my mother, striding off. "I'll get a pan." Then, from inside the broom-closet, "I need help. I can't reach. Where's Sam?" "Who?" said my father. "Oh, I don't know. He'll turn up. He always does." "Not always," I said. "True," said my father. "That'd be a turn-up for the book." This phrase came from his English childhood. I used to think he said "What a turnip for the book," and imagined a book fed on root vegetables, its pages like jaws but with no teeth, white mouths gumming the firm flesh, or nibbling with a soft squishy sound.

The above memory, or its reconstitution, ran through my head as I bent over digging up the last of the Yukon Gold potatoes, pulling up the dead stalks, tossing them onto the compost and forking in well-decayed cow and pig manure from the one farm left hereabouts. I was also thinking about the wonder of roots that grow in dark silence and secrecy, which led me to think of a lecture I once heard given by, I think his name was Tompkins, who said plants were sentient beings who loved classical music and had telepathic powers. He told the story of a plant who got visibly upset when an egg was cracked in its presence. Then I straightened up, washed my hands at the tap, and went to stretch my legs along the red dirt track that passed for a road. But the thing about living alone, retired, or forced into retirement, on a mountainside in the middle of the woods is not only that you tend to live in your own head but that you become very sensitive to the presence of people. You can sense them a mile away, like a dog, and you're always ill at ease, on the alert. Solitude does not come cheap and people can be scary. I hadn't talked to anyone in a while, not since I bought the manure. So I was rather alarmed to see someone coming toward me up the hill, getting bigger and bigger, but it wasn't the farmer's wife who I ran into once in a while walking her three giant mongrels, leashed, luckily for me. She had rather a strange outline due to the fact that she packed a Glock 17 handgun in her capacious bra. So no, I didn't recognize this growing outline of someone I'd never seen before. Now, I've found the key to keeping people at a distance is to fake it;

appear interested in them and they'll talk about themselves for ever. You don't have to say anything, but you do have to adjust to them. So when there was no avoiding him, I stopped, and he stopped too. Soon, he was banging on about the weather and then meteorology in general. I joined in, and from there we progressed to the wonders of science. I was almost glad I'd run into him, and shared how I'd been reading about how everything is just a rearrangement of molecules and genes. "A bit of this, a bit of that, quite by accident," I said, "just like our lives." "You a teacher?" he asked. "Don't you think we're all the same?" I said. "Even organisms in the soil, we're related. The key is evolution. All change." "You think?" he said. Then, "Makes sense. That's how they can put fish genes into tomatoes and—pigs, is it?—into whatever and who knows what into cows to increase the milk supply, and why not if, as you say, we're all the same which, incidentally, I do not believe. I mean, it's ridiculous, just look at monkeys and then look at us. Still, if we can do something I believe we should, like going to the Moon, if we really did, it's crazy, but all done for a purpose." "Yes," I said, "chains of molecules stretching out all round, taking different forms, including," I added, "you, me, all of us, even that guy in the cabin over that stone wall back down there in the woods who blasts away all day and half the night. Now I'm just as much for guns as the next guy round here," I lied, "but, well, moderation, consideration for others, right? Seems he was a Jersey cop who came up here after 9/11. He must be practicing for terrorists. Boom, boom, boom, exactly two minutes apart. As if they'd space their attacks every two minutes. And why are they coming at *him?* Crazy, huh?" "So you think you're safe now, up here ?" he said. "Not always," I said. "You think everything stays the same as it always was, nice and cozy up here?" "Not—" Before I could elaborate, he'd turned and marched back down the way he'd come, clambering over the stone wall at the bottom and disappearing into the woods. I too turned round and hastened back the way I'd come. When I got in the house I locked the door, or I would have if I hadn't lost the key. So I bolted it, twice. This is what happens, I thought, when you talk to people. They're confusing, and lead nowhere. A few glasses of Old Grand-Dad calmed my nerves a bit, but when I looked out the window I still felt a little woozy, as if there were a long drop over a cliff, but it was only the house about to fall a few feet into the pond, wavelets lapping at the porch where a forest had stretched a short while ago. I thought I heard a gun go off, but it was only the voice in my hair that said: It's all gone, or will be once I leave, everything, even my little painting, size of a quarto sheet, which the sun had bleached on the white wall, a winter scene all thin crosshatchings, white-out and magic marker, so faded you could almost see through it. If the forest was anything to go by, it would simply disappear and no one would have known or remember it had been there, not even me. It would not even be like ancient leaves in coal, beautiful before burning. I mean *nothing*, not even like the shadow of the solitary goose that just fell across the window, going off and away at a steep angle, so sharp it hurt, and scared me.

I stood there wondering if I'd ever be able to go back into the garden where I started all this, and thought about my father, who had been a great gardener, or would have been if he hadn't had a theory that the longer you saved something the more precious and powerful it became. This extended to seeds, with the result that nothing ever came up. Not even when he dumped on pounds of fertilizer, though sometimes the result was a giant vegetable, huge as those from Alaska, and just as useless. Luckily, I inherited my dad's passion for gardening and am always looking out for new things. This year, for example, I came across a device called called Parrot Flower Power. You

NOT THE REAL MARILYN MONROE

place it in the soil, synced to a smartphone via Bluetooth, and on an app the plant tells you what it wants, from vitamins and minerals to light and shade. It's like it talks to you, and makes you wonder what soil really is. Maybe Tompkins was right. Once I read somewhere that "the soil is a kind of loess," which I guess it could be in certain climes, but which I first read as "the soul is a kind of loss," which I preferred and which no doubt it could also be under certain climes and conditions. This led me to thinking about life itself, which I have to do carefully because when I don't my head gets hot and it feels as if my hair is on fire. Once, in a while, in fact, it is, but that's another story. A bottle of Chardonnay will put it out. And now, back to the soul. Audubon once said "I wish I had eight pairs of hands, and another body to shoot the specimens." Imagine that. It wasn't enough to shoot the living animal, but he wanted to shoot the ones he'd already shot and stuffed, in effect destroy their soul, which, in fact, in a way, he'd created. It boggles the mind and heats the hair. Well, what is the soul? And where? Some say it's in the chest or between the eyes, some say in a stone, some in the crown at the top of the head. Maybe that's how the halo arose, a ring of fire round the head. Maybe it's like the dove in darkness, or maybe like the watchman who goes out into the dark with his lamp to wash away the dark and stop it being *nothing*. Who knows? It could be the shape loss takes, something like the shadow of a shadow. The fact that you're left with a shadow-soul implies that the body is a kind of substance, and that's far from proven. Is the soul an afterimage, a version of something? Or is it simply the evidence of loss? If there were no soul what would be left, just the desire for soul? Maybe that's the key. Maybe the soul can be thought of as excess of being, as dark can be understood and experienced as excess of light. Or maybe, on the other hand, the soul is what defines the self, the way a poet said "the absence of rose is what defines 'rose.'" The way light follows when you look at it. Or maybe there is no soul, though my mother, who said she was part-Cherokee, claimed everything had a soul. If there is a soul, I've never sensed that it knows I'm looking for it. Everything knows when you look at it, no matter how you try to catch it out. I remember once seeing Andy Kaufman in a white suit picked out by a white spot rehearsing at the Theater Royal or somewhere. I knew who he was, of course, but I called out "Who are you?" trying to catch him off guard. But he knew who he was and what I was up to, and didn't reply. Still, I'd made my point. "What's held back is the most important," said the person who lives in my hair and who will remain anonymous, but who will always be there, the same, and I can call on him whenever I need, someone I can rely on, immune to the world, who always tells me the truth, or tries to, like Coyote's soul-sisters he kept up his anus, calling on them as required.

The Soul

1:
On the cereal box it says there are only 440 gorillas left. That can't be right. It also says they love to eat bananas—OK—and live in trees, which they don't. There's also a recipe for Easy Chicken Casserole that looks disgusting.

—*It doesn't look so bad,* says the soul.

2:
I took my laceless sneaker and killed the ant. A big black ant looking for crumbs under the table. An early ant. It took three smacks. It is barely spring.

—*Why did you do that?* says my soul.

3:
Where is Kearny, NJ? I know there are lots of Scots, hence the name. This letter's postmarked There, so I must know somebody. It sits propped against the cornflake box beside some flat batteries (AA).

—*Open it,* says the soul.

4:
A small white bear holds a black comb between its paws. My wife has written beside it: "The key to a good love is curiosity." I'm curious about who lives in Kearny, NJ, and why the bear needs a comb.

My soul says it's curious too.

5:
My soul also says it's not curious.
    It's just being supportive.

6:
Then it adds that—
    Wait. Time out to whack the ant again.
    (It moved).

7:
When I say the soul never changes I don't mean it's always the same. It goes through a series of colors, the soul, like a cuttlefish or flying saucer. What is color? A phase?
    Name? Note:
    Ask the soul.

8:
The ant's disappeared. I must have got it this time. Some philosopher wrote a book about what it feels like to be a bat. I wouldn't want to be a bat. Or an ant, totally unconscious, all scent and touch, a little black dream, driven.

9:
"On a sunny morning"—that's all I remember. And a headline from yesterday, "Upgrade Your Future. Be a Winner." I had an aunt named Win. I have another named Flo. I might have had an uncle named Eb, but that could have been a serial cartoon. The soul says not to set much store by names. Or words. I think it's wrong.

10:
Me, I've found I can live on nothing, without gas or driving belts, going on my own volition, like wind, all over. I say I could even be a fulcrum, the nothing in the middle that makes it go.
    —*A bit like the soul,* says my soul.

11:
"I was in that fog among the companionless...." Where's that from?
    —*Who knows? Words create, not describe,* says the soul, flicking through last week's "Book Review."

12:
I once found a large snake in the grass, I said. I called him Stanley, my father's name. I never saw him again.
    —*Lucky you,* says the soul.

13:
I feel a bit like a gyroscope, I say. Spins on any surface—
    —*No it does not.*

14:
Well, more or less, steady, can stand still, humming, great to watch, going so fast it's still. Only needs encouragement now and then and in theory could go on forever. Fulcrum. Centered wherever it moves. Pricking the mind. Gadfly. You know the drill. If it stood in one place it could be a firedrill, make fire. Illuminate.
    —*Or incinerate.*

15:

I left myself somewhere, I mean I left something somewhere. The face at the window, peeking in.

    —*That was me,* says the soul.

16:

I've learned the useless is a great thing to have. The abundance of the worthless can get you through. Also, that—

    —*Eat your cornflakes,* says the soul.

17:

I love my soul. It is water, it is glass, it is already awake even asleep. It fills space. It cannot wake. It has its own mind, it is not my mind. It is mirrors. It makes mirrors. It tangles and hangs there, among us. It goes by scent, by touch, by taste.

    —*It gets by,* says the soul. *If all was well we wouldn't need a soul.*

18:

Nothing in the envelope. It arrived empty with the morning paper and its full-page ad: "Luna y Cultura: Mexico City Capital en Movimento: Even Day Has a Different Night".

    —*Empty?* says the soul. *That's more like it. Now we're getting somewhere. Let's go.*

NEW YORK TIMES SUMMER FICTION

After years of renting in the city, we finally bought a house upstate. Today, I'm stroking my beard, looking down from the study window at my wife under the sugar maple, stretched out on her chaise-longue, on one side a can of insect repellent and on the other a glacial rock. She's reading a novel, and when I go down she tells me I should read the last thirty pages, though she knows I hate novels. From her background reading, she tells me that the author's father left when she was a child. That her mother never loved her. The author's father left when she was twelve, but when he returned at fifteen he raped her. The novel went from bad to worse and became something of a bestseller. Taking the book back upstairs with me, I promise to read it, though I know I won't. Instead, I outline a story of my own in which the father dies, making the mother a widow. It is the girl's sixteenth birthday and she is sitting under a maple tree, alone. She is staring at a glass of iced tea, and the diary which will become her autobiography is at her side. She is a spindly kid and wishes she had more flesh. She dips into her thoughts and comes up empty. Putting down her pencil, she gets up and goes into the house, down into the cool basement. She likes the idea of company, but can't bear to be with anyone for long. She reaches up and pull on a string attached to a naked light bulb. She goes to a corner by the old boiler and selects a book, *Spoon River Anthology*. She sits cross-legged on the dirt floor and begins copying into her notebook the preacher, the madam, the independent man. This is how she's decided to learn to write, the way students used to sit in museums and copy masterpieces. Later, in college, where she publishes the first part of her autobiography in the school mag, it will consist mostly of floods, fires, car and plane crashes, deaths and near-deaths, disasters and near-disasters. After college, she will marry one of her professors, a much older man with a beard, whose one book on Borges the librarian she admires. She continues writing herself, working for twenty years on an autobiographical novel. And that is where we leave her, one summer day, at a remote rented cabin upstate, where she is sitting under a maple, stretched out on a chaise-longue, on one side a gin and tonic, and on the other the *New York Times* Summer Fiction issue.

Doubling Down

He drives me in his Land Rover from the city to his shining-stone mansion that sits next to Wave Hill, surrounded by grounds that overlook the lordly Hudson. Lunch is delivered to a small elegant table down a long corridor by a small elegant maid. Medieval Italian paintings are on the wall, Persian carpets scattered on the polished marble floor. As we sip our wine, he tells me about the paintings, provenance and all. He talks about tapestries and carpets and icons, until it's time to enter a large room with more paintings, plus statues. He motions me to a large leather armchair. I sink in while he sits on the sofa by the roaring fire. El Greco looks on while he picks up the unopened envelope I'd sent weeks before, pulls the string, reaches in, pulls out a page at random, skims it, lays it down, asks if I'd ever gone ice-fishing. "Well," I say, "but that poem—" He lectures me on the finer points of ice-fishing before pulling out another poem, skimming, laying down. He does this a few times while I sit quietly. "You tend to write poems on subjects you know little to nothing about," he says. "Here"—he hands me the envelope and the pages. "Go over it and we'll talk later." Across the hall I see a room with half a dozen people at tables and chairs, rolled-up paintings on the floor, crates ready for shipping. A TV is on in the corner, but no sound. He leads me up the grand staircase to a small room on the second floor. I sit at a desk, reach into the envelope. I don't really know what I'm looking for. Two hours pass. Maybe I should look for things I know nothing about. I take a nap. Three hours. I need to pee, but looking for a bathroom, I might get lost. Finally he returns. "Let's go down to the drawing-room," he says. I don't ask the location of the bathroom because this is where I'm sure he tells me he's going to publish my book. "Your package, take it with you." We enter another room like a museum. The phone rings. I sit and lay the package down by the armchair. I hear a discussion about the price of Armenian carpets. He hangs up. "Armenian carpets," he says. "Hard to get out. Now where were we? Ah, yes. Let me show you to the bus stop. It's just across the street. And don't forget that." He says, pointing to the package.

On the bus I resolve to stop writing poems and concentrate on prose. But then, as the city engulfs us, I backtrack and double down. I'll stick with poetry, but only on subjects I know little to nothing about, and I would keep writing until I knew even less. Years later I would publish a collection of poems titled *Ice-Fishing*. It got good reviews.

Country Matters

I

At the Valley Picnic, Mostly Weekenders:

"Our pond has pollywogs, lots of them. Frogs too. And salamanders." "Newts. Our pond has minnows." "Our pond has trout that eat minnows. And pollywogs." "How can trout live in a pond?" "I put them there. Our pond's spring-fed. Two springs—" "We have two ponds. I dug both." "—so it's always cold, even on a hot day like this." "Ours always has a foot of warm water on top so it's never too cold." "We have two ponds." "Ours is always clear. It's amazing." "Ours has beaver." "Beaver? In a pond?" "Well, they dammed the stream near the pond. Sometimes they come over." "You'll have to clear them out." "Lead poisoning." "I saw a big—animal. This big, with a tail." "Muskrat." "You'll have to clear them out. They undercut the banks." "Rat? No!" "Muskrat, musquash. Indian word. Fur coats." "No." "Then what? Beaver?" "No, I don't know." "Mink." "Mink eat trout. I saw one near your place with a trout in its mouth. Across its mouth. Looked like a moustache." "I saw a mother mink and two babies running after her along our wall heading toward your pond." "No, not ours. Those Russians next door dug a small pond, no bigger than a bathtub, and put goldfish in it. Goldfish. They also stained the water blue and put in plastic lily pads." "They came after 9/11." "Us too." "I saw a heron there the other day." "We have two ponds, one high, one low." "You should see our bulrushes." "They're cattails." "Moses was born in bulrushes." "We have red-winged blackbirds in our reeds." "I can hear your bullfrogs all night long." "I once stepped on a spring peeper." "We had a pair of geese nest on our pond." "How lovely!" "I shot them." "Oh." "My wife almost drowned when she got wedged in an inner tube and the patch came off and it sank. I saved her." "It's true, he did." "I have to put a fence around ours. Cars keep driving up at night, local kids. Leave all sorts of stuff." "I know what you mean." "Do you own a gun?" "Ponds are good for the environment. They encourage wildlife." "You really shot them?" "I keep the algae down with zinc oxide." "Isn't that the stuff you put on your nose to prevent sunburn?" "That too." "You really shot them?" "We have two ponds. Drop by. I might dig another." "When we first bought our house we thought your pond was ours. We don't have a pond."

II

At Home:

—I've separated the tomatoes into those that'll need a week to ripen and those that are ready to eat. I'll put you in the ready-to-eat pile. —Did you wash the tomatoes in the bathtub? It's filthy. —No. The cow. —I read that Cioran once wrote something like *All I ask of my friends is that they do me the favor of growing old.* —I'm not your friend. I'm your husband. And I may be old but maturity is for spuds and tomatoes. I boiled up a few spuds the spade nicked. —The military prosecutor said Noica's work was *a subversive content, full of irony.* —What are you reading? Doesn't matter. I'll sing you a song. Yeats, I think. *I met her in the garden where the fraties grow.* —That's not Yeats. —Then how about Shakespeare? *If you were the yoni girl in the world.* —Put some clothes on. The hanging gardens. —Quick!

Get the watering can. Get it while you can. —You know, it says here that in our culture you only need to do one thing well, anything. What happened to the well-rounded man— person? —Put that iPhone down. You wouldn't put those on the internet, would you. Wait, I'm not ready. You know that Leon Golub painting, *How'm I doin'? Not bad, huh?* —That's Ed Koch. —Nice name, that. Molly Bloom. You know, digging up spuds here is hard work. The tree roots take over the soil and then pull back when you try to extract the spuds. Then they snap and send you tumbling arse over titfa. Right into the worms. You should see my fat worms. —I don't want to see worms. I'll see them soon enough. I don't like worms. Stop being morbid. —*I'm* being morbid? I'm proud of them, gorgeous creatures with blue or green stripes. And fat. —Talking of which, you could lose a few pounds, even though today is your birthday. —It is a load to carry, mortality. But lighten up. You're the yoni one for me. —Let go! Your hands are filthy!

E-MAIL

Das Ewig-Weibliche / Zieht uns hinan
—*Faust*

"Tuesday, 17 October, 67. 'Irene Romberg,' 6568180 (3245655, office)." I am staring out of my window on 5th Avenue, but when I look down at my desk there is this typed bit of paper poking out of a pile of legal briefs. Just that. By itself. I pick it up. Why? Who are you? Why all the quote marks? Is it a code? What's the code for? In case it fell into the wrong hands? "Romberg." Wasn't that the name of the guy who wrote "The Student Prince" and "The Desert Song" my mother used to love? I used to like it too. But I don't think "Romberg" was his real name. And why Irene? Isn't that Greek for something? Maybe the numbers translate to musical notation, diatonic, solfeggio, which comes out, for the first set, "la fa la do do do," which sounds a bit like "Lafcadio," but what's that zero? (And "67"—maybe a year?) If it's a song it's not much of a tune, certainly not up to the standards of the Sigmund Romberg I'm familiar with. And only two bars? What key would it be in? That might be the key to the whole thing. But no, that's not the way. "Irene Romberg," if you exist, as I'm sure you do somewhere in the mystery of time, I remember nothing about you, and I don't like that. All I have to go on is "Tuesday, 17 October, 67." 1967? Where was I then? Oh yes, Rome. At home in Greenwich that evening I checked the yellowing pages of old journals until I found Rome, where I'd gone to escape business school and become a novelist. I kept turning the brittle pages. I doubt you were the girl who sat next to me at the British Council lecture Mr. Robert Spaight gave on *Othello*, and who walked out at his remarks on Desdemona, thus missing his statement that Othello didn't have the dignity of leadership to be a Negro, and when he—Spaight—was in Manhattan he saw many Negroes who were light-skinned. If that was you, you also missed his claim that Othello was in fact a Muslim convert from Mauritius. But no, I don't think that was you. Maybe you were the girl with Barbarella features and mad blue eyes who'd just had an abortion and who put her bare feet on my pillow with a cold manufactured anger and threw her cigarettes on the floor but had to pick them up when her husband came in with an ice-cream cone which she accepted but had only eaten half when he shoved the other half in her face. No, that girl doesn't even have a name, or none I noted or can remember, or decipher. Others I can, so why be code for Bianca, Cristina, Anna who slept in a bathtub, Flavia with the Etruscan face, Pato the Irish girl who in the elevator punched me in the stomach and doubled me over, and who found being a woman "ridiculous," the other Irish girl who saw Paddy Cavanagh chasing the dustman's cart with a pail, the Australian girl who made her bikinis from cut-up mens' ties and the name tags from their shirts, Ursula the Swedish girl who modeled for *Foto Romanza,* and who knitted all the time, yellow wool on yellow needles, and who had a thyroid condition, Judith who "projected" and had a father complex and hysterics, Yael's girlfriend after he was murdered by Mossad, Penny Heath, my boss at the language school who I called Penny Lane and who had a thyroid condition and who called me the Walrus in the Beatles' song, Joan who talked incessantly of the Italian male's addiction to buggery and told me that after marriage she never saw her husband again, and the woman who told me how her husband in Vietnam shot a boy who was throwing a grenade at

163

him from a roof, and the lady at the British Council lecture on "Leisure" who told me not to use the word "buxom" ever again, Peppina in Procida, sister of Antonio who had spent eighteen and a half years in Procida jail for shooting an officer who had shot a pregnant woman while, it seems, he was really trying to shoot Antonio for having an affair with his sister, Elsa, or Luisa at Pompeii, 25 April, Liberation Day, or Occupation Day, depending on your point of view, Pamela, Graeme's mum, red face, short fat legs, José's mamma in Bolzano who begged the Brazilian military not to take her "unique son," Bici Valori who could never master one word of English, Polly Peabody at Roccasinibalda, Iris who lived just around the corner in Lungotevere, the rich American lady who was petting the gray tom who'd refused to move out of the way of a three-wheeler and whose swish companion whined that now she'd have to wash her hands? No, not these. But then who? Certainly not Natalia whose son I got to know briefly later, and not Jane Fonda's secretary who could only talk about being Jane Fonda's secretary, and not Eleanor whose book on Rome I admired but didn't know who her famous husband was. Maybe the girl with the gait of a ballet dancer whom I followed, kept finding and losing, through rooms, through dungeons. I felt we had something going as she sat at the base of the campanile but wait, that was Venice, so no. Maybe the beautiful Finnish psychiatrist who played the flute and who told me hardened criminals tend not to dream. Or La Donna Bonna, no, wait, that was where I ate lunch, Cristina from Sardegna whose father was a colonel in the *Carabinieri,* on the beach at Torvaianica, who wore a pony-skin coat, liked to eat little birds on spits and had fritti di cervello for dinner, or Miriam who said I was "deficient of a sense," or Lidia who owned a trattoria and who beat her boys if they didn't eat, and Ivanka—no, that was in another country, and besides. Maybe the girl on the balcony with short skirt and orange stockings, or Loretta the anarchist whose walls were thick with revolutionary posters and who sang *"Bruciamo il vaticano,"* well into the night, maybe Miss Fantini at NATO Defense College, Joan the sister of King John who was married to William II, King of Sicily—how did she get in here? No, you couldn't have been any of these, for various reasons, but if not, then who? Who are you "Irene Romberg"? I need to know. I need to clear things up. Time's getting on. I'm getting on. Are you getting on, are you the one who got away? The one who could have changed my life? God knows, it needs changing. I would give you my e-mail address but from way back then you wouldn't know how to use it, and you have no way of letting me know yours. Well, in any case, just in case, you never know, so here it is now:

Friday

The man pushed the woman up the embankment. Her feet slipped, but he caught them and shoved them up upward. Then he cupped her buttocks and heaved. She made it to the top, paused, then hauled herself up and over. He followed, stood and looked back at the blue-black river.

They walked through narrow streets past a church with an ornate front. Over the double doors were carved its abbreviated name and a date, in Latin, as well as the information in English that this was one of the churches mentioned in "Oranges and Lemons." He sang the song quietly to himself. It wasn't. And this wasn't the church they were looking for, which they found close by and entered.

The cavernous interior was almost filled, each bench, chair or pew occupied. There was a low hum of excitement. Where could they sit? Suddenly, through a gap between heads, he spotted two spaces on a bench along a wall. They moved fast, and squeezed in. Just in time. She took out a notebook and began to write. The organ pealed, the choir sounded off just as a large woman dressed in what seemed a gray trench coat stepped up into the pulpit. She silenced the choir. She gave another sign and they began again. When the hymn ended, a woman on the bench whispered excitedly, "She saved my life! I was nothing until I heard her! She made my life worthwhile! She—" "Ssh," he said. "We can't hear." But she continued. "All my life I've waited for this moment. You should have seen me before." "Shut up," said his wife. "I'm trying to write." The large woman in the pulpit continued her sermon, but gradually people began pushing chairs back, gathering up bags and coats, children, spouses as if they'd heard it all before. He turned to whisper to his wife, but she was not there. He stood up and saw her under a large, highly carved pillar deep in conversation with the woman they'd been sitting beside. His wife looked happy, talking excitedly, waving her hands. He turned away, tucked his head down deeper into his anorak, pulled up the hood, closed his eyes. People would think he was deep in thought.

He opened his eyes to the preacher striding about, her thoughts on love amplified throughout the great echoic space, now almost empty. He walked out into the night. The city was bustling but without much intensity. Something made him turn into an alley. A long light was spilling down a long staircase in a rather palatial building. He walked over and began to climb. He pushed open a door at the top. There was his wife, washing her long blonde hair over a deep sink. Without looking up, she said, "I was working on three different endings to this story. This is the only one that made sense." A young man came from the rear of the room. She turned her head and smiled.

The man walked back to his hotel until, passing a taxi-stand, he recognized the driver who had driven them from the airport and got into a conversation. "How much longer are you staying?" the driver asked. "Not long now," he replied. "I'm flying out on Friday." "This Friday?" "Yes, this Friday. Why?" "Nothing, mate. Just that Friday's a strange day to leave."

HAGIOGRAPHY

At fourteen, coming into myself, I tacked above my desk Bellini's *St. Francis in the Wilderness*, with its great cave and writing desk and him inspired gazing off and up somewhere and you're supposed to know or find out what he's thinking and what all the details mean for they don't mean just what they mean—that is, the rocks, cave and flowers are not just rocks, caves and flowers, the heron and ass not just themselves, and so on. Alongside, I put up Carpaccio's *St. Jerome and the Lion*, which had another writing desk and another ass and often the two paintings ran together and mixed, so I couldn't always remember where St. Jerome's lion went and which ass went where, but it didn't really matter since my two favorite saints fell into place in my mind while the narrative took its own turns with, for example, Jerome helping the lion while Francis, busy as usual caring for the sick, poor, leprous and mangy, still managed to communicate joyfully with all of nature while composing his *Fioretti* and keeping a serene eye on what went on, including the lion who by now had fallen in love with Jerome for pulling out that thorn from his paw, thus risking sharp teeth. Anyhow, I found out that some merchants stole the ass, and the lion, who was supposed to guard the ass, was accused of eating him, though he didn't, and was made to take the place of the ass carrying wood. In another version the ass ran away for reasons that were unclear and joined a camel train which the lion got accused of eating also, but that too turned out to be false. But the way I saw it, it didn't matter. It all came out the way it was supposed to, and there were even other ways they could have come out, and still can. Saints change, saints should not be static. And the same with their stories.

A Man's

acid to himself, forgetting what he is or what he's looking for, even the glasses on his face, he's looking for them, the slippers on his feet, he's looking for them too, when even looking's a gamble. There are always limits and limitations to confront. As for me, things often seem to be done by someone else. Point out a door and I can't bring myself to walk through. And my body, now aging, was always someone else's, bones, muscles, organs independent, reliable cells shipped out and weaker ones slipped in, until I'm all replacement, not just hips and knees, while memory makes its own minefield to play in with the familiar who greets me each morning after a night gnawing at itself, stomach still flipping like a fish on wet stone. I'm slowly drawn into day's vacant glass, looking off into distance that bites like steel on steel, into its shiny emptiness, less and less, air opaque as water.

The Clown in the Elevator, the Fool in the Machinery

Walking across Brooklyn Bridge, heading east, on a day when the traffic has been banned, something makes me look up. I stop and point. The sky is changing. Great coiling scoops, then black broken lines inside them rolling like the lines on slow, disappearing roads. When I look down, people are staring at me, then looking up, then back at me, until over the bridge-crest a procession appears. A woman in a tall pointed hat like Merlin is in the lead, dancing, prancing. With a large wand, she points skyward calling out, "Clouds, gorgeous clouds by the fabulous, the beautiful, the fantastic—" Her voice almost drowns out everything, young women blowing on fifes, beating drums, young men working puppets, followed by clowns cutting up, some on stilts, and court jesters, fools in cap and bells. Some people get caught up in the swing, while others look puzzled and some seem angry as the sky expands, overwhelming. Suddenly, bursts and bangs like fireworks, and a huge cloud forms like one of Macy's Thanksgiving Day balloons covering everything, billowing out so we are all under it like chicks under a hen until we're sucked up into its airy grand hotel where all the elevators are out. So I run down the stairs, sometimes sliding down banisters. When I get to the bottom the cause of the breakdown is announced over the intercom. "Some clown is trapped in an elevator," it says. "And a fool is gumming up the machinery. This is very serious. This is not a test. This is not a game. We cannot run things like this. We need help." So I sit

171

down on the bridge. The procession has passed. Spreading out the parts of this story around me, I begin to sort through them carefully. Logically, I start to figure it all out.

The Contortionist

Watch me, he says, this limb, for instance, that bends until it's nothing, or this shoulder I dislocate, or the integuments and tendons I stretch and twist, flail about so they lose focus, my spine flexible to a fault I can turn hoops on, or wheel myself around, whirl like a lariat and vanish "before your very eyes," as they used to say—have you ever seen anything quite this before, can you believe your eyes as I twitch and turn to drumrolls, build to a climax and to cap it all off, often in medias res, quick as a flash, drop off the stage and slip away, leaving you all wondering what you've seen, looking about, *where is he?* until you decide OK, that's that and leave, though I hope you'll come back, but most won't, preferring to seek out the clean lines of the sword swallower, the flair of the fire eater, the bearded lady, or the man who twists balloons into sausage dogs.

THE DWARF

There is no such thing as a "thing," a word meaning a "gathering," a kind of parliament, a place for play and decision, voices clumping, clotting. Any direction there is only another direction somewhere else. A thing does not stay. A thing fragments so it is not a "thing." But does all this matter so long as you express possibility in the confusion?

As I was thinking this, acting it in my head, for, as Descartes said, "the mind is a kind of theater," I realized I was working through a vague memory of a house with many outbuildings. Certain people were there, but not what they did or said, nor why the house was the way it was.

So I added what was done or said but never questioned why. But why, I wondered, were the people variations of other people, in effect spirits, tangibly present and absent at the same time. I wasn't aware of what they'd say before they said it, but I knew once they'd said it I'd heard it before. All this was proof enough for me, if proof were needed, that the world itself is spirit; tangible, fleshy even, but beyond that it is either nothing or something that informs and animates, therefore I'll call it spirit so I can get along in my quest.

*

Like Alice, I am "very fond of pretending to be two people," or even more, different kinds, be what Sartre called "the obligation ... to be what we are not." And sometimes, I think I am a fractured thing that leads elsewhere to other conclusions, especially when I wonder about the consciousness an object or thing possesses, especially when I wonder what it must be like to be that object or thing. If that object is judged to be non-conscious, however, I can do no wondering at all. What would be the point? In effect, it hardly exists at all, so to wonder what it's like being that object would be to concern myself with a question different from any scientific or practical question, unless I went in the direction of the science of imaginary conclusions, and even then I'd only be playing about.

Which explains why, perhaps, when I was thinking about what it was like to be the kind of person called a dwarf, a group of them chased me. As I dashed by him, an artist looked up from his easel and pointed to a mansion over the hill. I ran through its open door. Inside, I heard a voice telling me to climb up under the false ceiling, which I did. I crawled through the dirt and dust until I came to a hole in the wall that overlooked a courtyard with a large pool for bathing, but which was now murky. I stuck my head out and looked for the dwarfs, but there were none. Soon, I'd forgotten about what I'd decided it was like to be a dwarf and dropped down, judging that the pool looked substantial enough to walk on. What is it like to be a pool? I thought, as I carefully walked around the rim, then ventured further out. The water held. But when a sandal came loose and drifted down into the deep I lost confidence, panicked and dashed back to the edge like one of those frilled lizards—a Jesus lizard, I believe it's called—that runs on water. I stood on the side, wondering why I had even bothered to wonder about dwarfs in the first place when from the mansion I heard a sweet voice. Throwing off the remaining sandal, approaching cautiously, I looked through one of the diamond-shaped panes. There stood a dwarf with no arms, no lower limbs to speak of, dancing and singing, surrounded by all sorts of instruments which from time to time he took up and played. He also did magic tricks with handkerchiefs and scarves, balls, playing cards, and boxes. I was astonished to see him make birds appear from nowhere and fly about before vanishing. But most astonishing of all was to have the pane I gazed though become a magnifying glass so I could make him out take a quill between his stumps, dip it into ink, and start painting. But instead of actual lines, he used miniscule letters of the alphabet so they looked like lines to produce portraits of things and people. Slowly, I realized he was also making a portrait of me, which, unfortunately, no matter how hard I tried, I could not read. He looked up and, waving his stumps in my direction, left the room in a cloud of birds.

I stepped back, turned around and saw a bicycle leaning against a wall. I took it and rode off, thinking about what I had just seen. When I reached the village, deciding I needed the cup that cheers but does not inebriate, I leaned the bike against a wall. I was about to go into the tea-shop when, ahead of me, a distinguished-looking older gentleman dropped a valuable-looking cane shaped like a St. Stephen's cross but missing one arm. I picked it up and went in. He sat in a corner. "Yours, I believe," I said. "It's not mine," he replied. I left it with him and sat in another corner. By the time I went back out, someone had stolen my bike, which, of course, was not mine.

My bare feet were frozen now and I had no means of transportation. So I decided to think what it might be like to be a plane. How do planes fly? Science tells us, but it doesn't seem right. And even if one understands, it is still very hard to believe. To be a plane is always to be at the whim of vagaries such as design, weather, terrorists. You don't have a mind of your own. But then, you might ask, does a bat? Well, I imagine it certainly has more than a plane. Have you ever seen a plane decide to turn in midflight and snag a fly? No, but then I suppose you've never tried to ride in a bat. I find this line of thought unprofitable. I have enough problems thinking what it's like to be me rather than worry about planes, dwarfs, whirligigs, Praxiteles, bats and all the other circus animals. But then I remembered Lévi-Strauss' dream which, he said, was to talk like a bird. That, I decided, would be something. And not impossible. That dwarf might help. He had the birds.

ANONYMOUS

For proof I stop to consult a mirror. I emerge with what's left or missing, not me, but someone else I decide to travel as, without maps, without history, anonymous. I'll leave with just the necessities this someone would take though it's late, very late, and I'm old. So I go, accompanied by wraiths who walk beside me, more air than matter, more matter than me. When we stop for the night I reel in a gray evening that's about to swallow a few old familiar fishing shacks and bright patches that look like miracles but turn out to be white paint splashed here and there. As light fades further it's like a badly re-wound demo tape skipping patches and playing itself out. But before it all goes, under a faint moon I can make out a wherry tampering with the horizon, loosening it so it arrives here as a line of flotsam planks worked by ship-worms into stalls from a cathedral. As small waves jostle at my feet and tiny crabs head out like multiple magi across the sand, clouds start to fill the world to the rim with snow as anonymous as me.

CRY THE BELOVED COUNTRY

I do not know this government and will not recognize it. It is immoral, immodest, and impecunious. As long as that monstrosity stands at these gates I shall be forced to conclude that it cannot be moved. At that point, I shall order the immediate seizure of all the last vestiges of decency. I call upon you all to close ranks, praise God and save the king, while we raise high the roofbeams and ask for a new estimate on the cedar shingles that will cap this noble edifice of marble, dahlias and democracy which is the cornerstone of this gruesome constitution of this great land of ours and which will prove the grindstone of our future, unless, if or until we allow free passage to the crowd of worthy harebrained schemes which I will fight to the last to defend in the interests of free expression to turn the members' billiard tables into ladies' washrooms and the ladies' washrooms into a place for all who identify as any sex whatever. All opposed, well, they shall not pass, though this is not the time or place to go into the logistics of hot water except to say that at this end of the faucet there's more than meets the eye. As St. Paul said, there's a lot more where that came from. So, dearly beloved, if it means that we men will never again be allowed to pee on our own billiard tables, then I move that we call upon the honorable Almighty to witness that His book is being rewritten to a foreordained menu of self-righteousness and plain vengeful vindictiveness on the part of the females in our society—God bless them—whose uppity hand is not being seen in everything. The righteous *shall* enter the kingdom of heaven, to be sure, but by that time it'll probably be a Socialist

Soviet Republic or Chinese satellite or Israeli redoubt or
Iranian oil-derrick in the sky. Now I didn't bring you here
this afternoon, folks, to effect a break with any member of
the NATO alliance. I'm no last Trump. Not today. Tomorrow
maybe, if I can find out who stole my quorum. Which reminds
me. There is overmuch sinning in these parts. Down the valley
a ways we have two good examples which shall be swept away.
The names of these places is slidedown and termorra. Real dens
of vice, iniquity and overpriced admissions. They even mark
the chess pieces and load the dominoes. Ain't no one ever going
to crack that egg, I hear you say. Well, say I, we'll see.

*

You figgerin' stayin' in town long, stranger? The handsome
stranger stepped back, giving his gun-belt a slight twist to
the left, for his Colt .45 was hitting him in the balls when he
swaggered. He threw his chewed Marlboro to the dry dusty
street that was to be the last witness to the philosophical
spectacle of two gentlemen of the saddle putting their trust not
in chariots and not in horses but lead bullets at twenty paces
lodging in the aorta's left ventricle or right earhole. He was
handsome, sure. Lean and raw-boned from sitting on a horse
whose spine was a razor-blade. When he spoke, the other man
threw himself at his feet and groveled spectacularly for a few
moments. Then he got up. When he'd brushed himself off, the
handsome stranger took his Colt .45 and shot him through the
left earhole to teach him a lesson. I am the Yankee Kid, he said,
You all go home now and look after your wives and kids. That
was what made America great at the beginning and will make
America great again. Law and order and the right to bear arms
but not arm bears, men being men and women being women.
That way we know where we are. And if elected I make this
promise. At no time during my term of office will I engage

in cunnilingus or in any illegal activities whatsoever which I can't claim as tax-exempt or charitable institutions. When (if) I get caught, I promise not to tell who assassinated Chou El Lai and Fidel Castro. I promise that half the millions I get for my memoirs written from minimum security will be devoted to the charitable institutions that care for indigent congressmen and their indigent clients. And I swear by the Holy Book that all I have said is the truth and nothing but a close proximity thereof, so help me, Hi Ho Silver. I swear by all those fingers on all those triggers in a million silos deep in Indian country that will, if necessary, bring peace and prosperity in self-defense. As you all know, we only attacked when our hand was forced and there was no other recourse but to retaliate and sink their country as a preventative measure after our wall had failed to prevent mass migration. In other words, by taking evasive action before we were attacked meant that the initial strike preempted their undoubted desire to launch their missiles at a country grown soft and flabby with the effects of great prosperity, irregular exercise, and irregularity of behavior. They were never more wrong, though there are not enough of them around now to know it.

*

I pledge as warden that I will poison all the cats, flatten all the mice, and any cockroach found consorting with prisoners will be severely dealt with, no appeals. If there is any more noise over there I will have to come over and break both your arms. If there is any more noise I shall have to paralyse a few of you. Anyone wanting to leave the country will be walled up alive, except those bastards I throw out. Anyone saying a bad word about his mother or father or grandparents of either persuasion will be consumed by the latest subway turntable during rush hour. Let no one harbor such a person, for they are liars and turncoats. In our democracy there is room for everyone but not for those we deem undesirable. We will wait for history to pass a decision and make it stick through school and college textbooks, competitions for our annual songfest competitions, which I shall judge, and the edicts of businessmen and politicians in silk shirts. *Vade mecum.* I will make you fishers of men, like the three little fishes that swam and swam right over the dam, three little fishes, father, son and holy mackerel, yes, with these fish I thee wed while hell's black agents to their prey do rouse. If you can stand this no more then look elsewhere. Love it or leave it. If you want dynamite go to Vegas. Blowing up houses and burning them to the ground is probably a psychic or psychotic manifestation of the right-to-life movement or maybe too much free choice. I have been living under the threat of expulsion, actually I have been expulsed. With the gates closed, I have looked back many a time and seen the serpent glittering with the sheen of his own deep knowledge. I had hoped that by the sweat of my brow I could move into his skin, but no. The Milky Way is his spine, his scales clouds, earth his belly. I look forward to how it will all end when we shall all be as gods and know nothing.

III

THE ECHO'S UNDERCURRENT

I:

Birds come back in their cries over bauchy snow. Six a.m. light carries the little stream from the quarry melt faster and faster past the empty bird feeder that waits for the child to fill it from a jar just a bit bigger than her potbelly. But she is still asleep, wrapped like a newborn beside her mother, snoring like a soldier, dreaming perhaps of the icy stream she washes her doll in to get her ready for the King of the Mountains and the people in the purple sky she sings about who say, "You should be grateful for what we've done for you." I pad round the silent house, cold creeping into the small of my back. I pick up her drawings with their bug-eyes and feet on backward. "Is it fair to expect the truth from a child?" she's asked. The silence is so constant it almost goes unnoticed. I hear as silence one bird almost overhead calling after the flock already in the pine-stand. It says everything is to be needed less and less.

II:

First peepers, then boom of bullfrog. The robin in rust sits on the empty feeder looking around for her last year's nest where the maples' twigs have turned red as their flowers that spill over the newly-turned garden. I watch her move along the stone walls, under the huge ancient battered line-trees, branches big as trunks, some cracked open and fallen, others fallen and lodged among others even larger that still push out red flowers delicate as orchids. But she is not looking at them, and not back at me, on her way to the abandoned house to visit the lone carp floating all gold through empty water that a few weeks back was weight-bearing ice. Circling, rising, reaching up, dropping down.

III:
The sky's spectrum has shrunk as I walk home by the water's edge. I can't stop thinking about furniture when all I want are a few lines by Rilke. At my feet, deer prints cross the mud. There is a bark in the sky from a lone goose. There is an island in the lake you can't really see, but as it heaps up or crouches you feel it.

IV:
Small creatures in the back field are burrowing through the thatch of dead grass, shaking it. Below them, roots are hoarding their hard kernels of fire. We watch a deer trembling in thin snow, listen to one bird whistling like broken water until it leaves. She wonders, pointing to the sky, where the bird went, and tells me a story she'd read where someone was forgotten when everyone left for a new home in one of the cold points overhead. "Shall I sing you your favorite song, how summer is a garden you wake in?" She nods.

V:
Bright fields offer a kind of dream. Trees waves. We sit under one. I watch a child push a paper boat where the current clenches and swirls. A kite attached to a thin arm pretends to be free. My daughter, almost too brown for her thin body, is listening to the goldenrod, a paper butterfly pressed on each of her cheeks. When we get home two sulfur moths are clinging to the broken screen door. When we approach they climb into nothing, and take off.

VI:

The house endures, wood warped, glass askew in a trance acute as absence. A sort of duress here keeps things in place, things whose urge is to be something or somewhere else. The door's still open on its broken hinges. There is nothing to impel shadows forward, nothing to make anything else, or more, nothing to crush the light that oppresses like darkness pushing in, pushing everything else out.

VII:

I'd cut through grapevines, heaped piles of leaves, dug. Scattered her multi-colored seed necklace, scattered flowers. She used to hear the crows at night and cry. She was a drumming so light, a brief summer's child, a small rain. I look through the window, up the steep trail to see if the mountains would make doves for her again. Today it's rained slush. My wife clears the table. "How's the well?" I run my hand along the back of the cold metal chair. A blue shadow creeps under the door from the family graveyard. "It might work. Tomorrow. I'll fix it." Go to the door. What sun's left drops. The northern star will come, a blind thing walking high where snow still fills boundaries. Then I hear her, knees drawn to her chest, folding herself up on the worn floor in the spare room. Like each night. Facing the rear wall.

VIII:

A girl appears, frost on the backs of her hands. Her father just sits there. He still thinks death can be fixed. On a chair beside the fire she combs her hair, whose brightness shores up the world. A cold breeze rises from her ankles and a vein shrinks into itself. He turns away. In this ghost town the shadows won't let you see much. He thinks this might be part of his education, part of an experiment everybody is in on except him. He's supposed to see things from a different angle, but he's hoping against hope for the girl to get up, brush the frost from her wrists and the backs of her hands, the frost that burns him, still.

IX:

The land beyond the gates begins to heave. Morning's tide is rising. Light catches in trees. Veins open and fever spreads over the various outbuildings behind me. The red hen drums her wings. A pilot goes in circles above the black willows. The white horse clatters in the corral like a spirit in a glasshouse. I can feel the nerve in the bone's core. The mind is victim here. Deer turn into reeds. The wind unwinds again, hissing. Soil scatters from loose sods over this tall shadow, my caricature. A whisper in the willow. I cannot move. Each morning is like this. I retreat into the house, but under floorboards: leaves, snow, blood, bones.

X:

The room was changed when the wind died. My wife went to the window, opened it. Together we watched the willows, the alfalfa fields, all suddenly still. A girl walked up the hill, paused to lean against the barn. On the fence in front of her a hawk sat. She turned to look up at the window, then left. As she walked her feet made little puffs of dust. We watched until she turned her head before crossing the river and heading for the reservation. Far away, a tree opened full in a sun burst. I wanted to shout, but here the sound one person makes is translated almost at once so you can lose yourself in it, or the darkness that springs from the echo's undercurrent.

XI:

A sudden flaw of wind blows the dust away. Pollen lifts in clouds while I recall her down by the creek sitting on a rock, looking over her shoulder at something that glints, metallic. She has left her dress crumpled on a rock. She has a feather in her mouth, gripped between her teeth. I feel her breathing, though she doesn't see me. She is already turning to memory, something not quite there, more there than ever.

Winter Suite

1:
On the mountainside the fox moves in, hungry enough to feed on thistles. In the chill below him a goshawk cuts across the space it defines. Here you are close to yourself as sky widens, a window expanding into you.

2:
All around me they circle, move off, return as if not sure. Then they are away, beating against the sky that tries to hold them back but which they skitter through like kids. After I watch them go, I consult my calendar with its mottoes in the margins from Poor Richard stressing moderation, delaying pleasures, retraining curiosity, playing it safe.

3:
I brush something black off the bed and onto the floor. Brittle and shapeless, it retains its shape. I rise, brew coffee, black, and from my window watch the vole's tracks zipper the snow beside mine and remember a story by Poe in which someone ended on an ice-floe and floated off. Here the mind looks out and the mind looks back, not what I want, more another mind altogether, maybe the vole's that keeps its shape, focused in its tracks, each foot the same distance apart, aimed, since it only knows what is useful.

4:

I wipe my glasses, think what I've become, as I light the dusky window and clear the disordered table. I take down a book. I have become someone to look right through. In me the lost and dead rise like heartburn. What good are they? They scatter with whistles of despair in rain that's left a few lights in trees. I turn the remaining pages fast, as if I were a character wanting to see who makes it to the end.

5:

Exhausted, the cows are spent torches. Back in the barn they didn't want to leave, their feet make flat wet sounds on the concrete, and they sigh. There are things I need to know but a cow is not a maxim. Things are not signs though I read this snow as a blank page. It is a hard time, the world empty, articulate, complete and equivocal.

6:

Wind still out of the north. Stars still sharp. As you try to sleep you can hear the red shift as it passes like an express train, which is how you understand the un-understandable in a night hinged and squeaking in winds that push it about and you start to float away, nothing to hold you back, and see a child in a greenhouse trying to understand flowers opening to the echo of star-shine and the moon's bright scent, caught and held, an ocean away.

7:

Tart taut stars shut off the deer as she shifts her weight on the ice. You can see right through the ice. This is the newest copy of a copy that seeps back and all around, being shaped by everything, a chord ending with a note from another chord dying deep as the deepest sky waiting with figures to be composed and you remember how on Lindisfarne we used to catch rabbits by sending a crab into the deep burrows with a lighted candle fixed to its back.

Praxiteles

He had just found a baby-sized black female headless statue in the small surf, being rolled along the beach of small pebbles and stones, as if the waves themselves had made her, were making her, wearing her down, making her up. He had lost his keys, but he hadn't lost his raft. Wedging the statue under one arm, he flailed at the waves with the other, and was soon aboard again. It is hard to imagine why he would go to such trouble. But perhaps he was planning to place the headless statue beside his Aphrodite, in some spirit of commentary. Or he may have been planning to set it up elsewhere, with or without a head, and call it, e.g., *The Black Headless Aphrodite,* or just *The Black Aphrodite.* Or, since the statue had been rolled just about sexless in the surf, he could have been about to use it as a prototype of his bronze *Apollo Lizard-Slayer.* Or it will become the child of *Hermes With The Child Dionysus In His Arms.* In which case he'll add a little phallus, small, almost invisible, tasteful. Or he'll make it into something none of us could possibly foretell. Or just leave it the way it is, and if it is ever found nobody will know its history. But this is for sure. Praxiteles was planning to keep it from the bright paint of Nicias. It would stay black. Black is an absolute.

There are dogs released onto the beach, but too late. In any case, it is the nature of dogs on beaches to be easily distracted by such things as sticks. And these dogs are no exception. They watch the raft float away, bark a lot or a little at the waves, attack them, and retreat from them, hump and mock-hump each other. Dogs generally do not deal in surprises. They

Brian Swann

play remarkably few variations on genetic melodies. But the interesting thing is how seldom we tire of their actions, unless the object of their humping happens to be our leg, for example. And in such cases, we draw the line. But these dogs are now doing something unusual. They look uneasy, confused. They begin to wheel and snap at things we can't see. Then they all turn and scurry off the beach. To be sure there are startling shadows of light everywhere, and the sea is as responsive as a mirror with a voice. Perhaps it is this voice they hear that confuses them, or those blinding shadows that upset their black and white world which goes by clearly defined opposites. They act as one.

Praxiteles was known for his taciturnity. His wife was always noting that she had never had a good conversation with him. "I long for a good conversation," she'd say. Praxiteles came to hate the word "conversation." He never used it in conversation. "Talk" was good enough for him. It didn't imply more than one. He preferred to think of himself as the sum total of his deeds, the res gestae. When thoroughly exasperated, and only then, he would say, "I don't give a Phrygian's fart for all your words," and then lapse into silence. He thought of himself as the sum of things done.

And what he was doing now was paddling. By the time he reached home, the unusually warm sun of late autumn had dried him off. He was about to carry the statue to his studio, but his wife saw him first. Euthynia was once more calling him to account, insisting on a dialogue, a sense of community, some verbal play of mind, some engagement, some history, some *conversation,* for Hermes' sake! "When are we going to have friends, when are we going to the theater, when are we going to have a new house…?" Once, on a gathering trip, Praxiteles had seen her face float up through the clear water of the Gulf like a crystal shadow, a glass embossed shield. It dissipated before

194

it could burst on the surface. She, who long ago had been his model for *Aphrodite of Cnidus*, for *Niobe of the Tears*, and other lost or, worse, misattributed masterpieces. Even, maybe, now he came to think about it, for *Eros*.... Under his breath he told her to get back to the women's quarters. He said, "I've got water in my ears. I can't hear."

He managed to make the studio without her following. He sat the statue down carefully. Where the little head should have been, he laid a wreath of dead olive leaves. Then he left the studio and went for a walk. The wind felt like water. The sun beat down like rain. And yet there was a bite in the air and something like the smell of snow.

He found himself at the gymnasium. Stripped, he made a good figure still. He watched the young men making each muscle and sinew subservient to the will, while their bodies raced ahead under their own steam, each into its own future. Blood. He looked down at his hand. There was blood on his hand, on his body. His hand. But how? He retraced his steps. They led to a razor in his gym bag, where he'd rummaged about feeling for the lock and key to his locker. He'd found neither lock nor key, so he'd left his sandals and tunic vulnerable. His sandals were gone. "Look in the lost bin," said the attendant. "If it's lost how can I—oh, I see." When he looked, Praxiteles found more blood. Somebody had been there before him, dripping blood. Or had it been himself? Was it his blood? He remembered a similar situation some time before.... Taking from the bin a piece of bloodstained cloth, Praxiteles stanched the wound. He had lost many sandals in his time, and many keys to many locks. Wrapping his chiton about him, he crossed the street barefoot to the hardware store where he cornered a black-browed man, wrinkled, looking older than his years. A slave from one of the offshore islands, probably, or an ex-ally recently annexed. Praxiteles followed, forming an expression of his purpose in his

195

mind. Then he got angry. "Why are you here then if you don't know how to help customers?" The man grunted like another species. "I'll talk to the manager!" Praxiteles threatened. But the man had gotten one of his fingers stuck up his nose, and so the threat meant little as his head and hand wiggled and shook. Praxiteles carried out his threat nonetheless. "Name's Demetrius," said the manager, sticking out a mitt. Recently freed, thought Praxiteles, as Demetrius wiped his brown nose on the brown sleeve of his tunic. "I only brought in this key for size. It was in my gym bag. I wasn't trying to buy a lock to fit it. I need a new lock *and* key." "Yeah," agreed Demetrius. "I'll fire that little creep. He gets like this from time to time." Praxiteles knew there would be no firing, but he went along. When he got the lock (and accompanying key) he decided to cut short his day and return home. He remembered the little statue. By the time he got home, he might have some plans for it.

As he walked still barefoot, down the dusty road lined with the gray and twisted trunks of olives, and a few twiggy persimmon trees, their fruit blazing still, he felt the blood batting in his ears, like a great tide, a tidal wave of red made of smaller waves of red, relentless, about to crash through his skull and leave him floating on it, floating away.... When he reached his house he sat down on a stool by the window. Fence staves split from the trunks of fir and pine marched across his small portion of the Attic plain. A tall half-fallen tree-trunk lay across some of the staves, striking a number of them out like a primitive account, or ten years gone by on the wall of a prison cell. He turned and looked back into the room, seeking to reset his eyes on something familiar, something he'd made; his *Satyr Pouring Wine,* perhaps, or the same libidinous fellow *Resting.* But they weren't there. Damn the slave girls, he thought. Always dusting and never returning.

He closed his eyes, and stood up. His finger hurt. His head

hurt. He collapsed into his large wooden chair by the long dinner table. It must be dinner time, he decided, though there was nobody around. In the yard, a rooster gargled with four notes. A dog made an attempt at a howl. One of the slaves in the distance called out in a foreign tongue as she was being chastised for some transgression. Praxiteles became aware of the chip and chink of hammer on chisel. Cephisodotus and Timarchides, his two sons. On the table there were some peanuts in a kylix and some mixed fruit jelly in another.

Suddenly, Praxiteles stood up. Outside the window, branches were broken off, as in winter. Each branch was plastered with snow. The staves were traced in white as they moved off, and there were patches of snow on the dust. Off in the distance the mountains glistened like marble from Naxos, marble from Paros.... Parian marble melting under the hands of dear Scopas, dead these ten years—no, more. The snow startled him to attention. He looked down at his hand. No scar. He thought he might be in the wrong place. Or maybe the time was wrong. It all depended. He sensed the presence of women. This was a woman's place. But there were no women. He rested his head on his hand, and slowly a dream came back, a dream of a few nights back, perhaps, or longer, a long time ago. A baby girl was falling down a slope, and he couldn't save her. He held out his arms, as if in supplication, as if he wanted her to save him. But she passed clean through. He didn't know, he wasn't sure, if he should have grabbed her. So he didn't. Maybe, he thought, maybe she wanted to fall. And she did, in large bounces, until she split her spine on some rocks, and knocked her head off.

A door slammed. He snapped to. Maybe the wind. He looked out the window again. Fat flakes were settling. A voice from somewhere deep in the house. A woman's voice. He became aware of the books on the dining table, books in shelves along the wall. Women's books. Only books by women. He knew that each night for as long as he could remember he had slept in a woman's bed. A friend had taught him how to die with dignity, alone. There were photos of women on the walls where there were no bookshelves. There was an album on a small table. "First Summer," "First Winter." He spelled out the captions with difficulty. "First Chiton," "Trip to Argos," and so on. He unbent, and saw on another small table another book. "Works of Praxiteles," he spelled out. He turned the pages. Mostly second-rate stuff. Not him at all. None of the real stuff. Only *some* pieces were labelled "attributed to." The only one he would have acknowledged, *The Eros at Thespiae,* that page was blank. There was nothing there. No, wait. Floating up from the depths, a baby-sized black female headless form, arms out, mouth open, calling, calling ...

Whirligigs

I am filled with rubbish, but since I'm all blocked up and can't think, how would I know? I'm in way over my head; everything is over my head. My eyes are glued shut and my ears are stuffed. From deep inside where once I kissed someone good morning and another good night there's a rumble. Listen, what can you hear? Something like the swishing inside the womb, a dog doing a backstroke, then a giant sucking sound, a plughole draining a bathtub, so now in your clogged state you have to make sense of it all, even as it continues to get stuck and backs up like grains of sand in the narrow neck of an hourglass. You feel like the hourglass but there's nobody around to turn you over, and who can think while standing on his head, everything just as bad if not worse than when you were standing on your own two feet? Maybe a stray tornado will come in handy, inject some substance, even if it means setting us all about our ears in order to have us stand on our own two feet, know what's what and what's going down, even if it seems random, a blur, the way whirligig beetles on a still pond look crazy dashing and spinning about but in fact they must know what they think they're doing because they keep doing it. It's hard to keep watching without going a bit dizzy as their raft, the shimmering mat, pulls the surface tension into them and you don't dare take your eyes off them as they skate over whatever muck lies beneath while the water reflects whatever lies on top and if anyone should ask you what you're doing you won't feel like telling them for if they can't see it for themselves what is there to describe or reveal?

A BIRD IN A GILDED CAGE

"The bruise of light, the yeasty blow of flowers." I don't know if that is a quote or all my own. Does it really matter so long as you express possibility within your confusion? (I think I used that line before, but it bears repeating.)

*

Faces come through the bars. The afterimage of bars gives them bars to come through. I draw the curtain as best I can across the panes, "those transparent things through which the past shines"—I'm pretty sure that's somebody but I don't know who. Nabokov, maybe, or Paz who said "man spies on himself." I certainly spy on myself and catch myself if not doing all sorts of things, then thinking them, which is a kind of doing. What can I see? A heart broken in a time of going, bodies ravaged in a season of bountiful fruits, time itself engulfed in intoxicating offices where "the flower of the heart hath burst open, the flower of the night" (*Florentine Codex,* Book 2). I do not have more than I thought I enjoyed. Even from a distance, the steps' crimson silk, the flash of light on flint, the cold wind whistling through a rack of skulls, can there be gardens and cars lighter than shadows "where mounds of human heads recede in a mist?" Can I hear my blood singing in its prison as the sun pulls me out of myself to look at a mangy cur sniffing the steps for what is still seeped in there? The possibility that you do not exist opens up all sorts of possibilities.

*

A slather of stars where everything seems to stand still, and yet "so many were absent that if one more hadn't come it wouldn't have been able to get in." Does it matter who said that? Or even if anyone did, or what it means? I thought as I was working through a memory until I realized it wasn't a memory, a dream, maybe, adding what was done or said but never questioning why. Certain people were there but not what they did or said, and never questioning why, nor why the house they were in was only an elaboration of itself, though I knew that what they said I'd heard before, making me wonder about the consciousness anything possesses whenever you wonder what it might be like being that thing, even if it's considered non-conscious as you speculate about something that is not available to scientific, positivistic question or inquiry, something seeming rational but delirious, like my grandmother riding a penny-farthing furiously on the Town Moor in a full-blown skirt, a bird-cage hanging from her handlebars, singing, "I'm only a bird in a gilded cage."

RAIN

At the center are the seeds; at the center
is the engendering fire.
                    —Gaston Bachelard

A gentler rain started late in the afternoon. A Waldensian
rain conducive to the quiet virtues, simple; something like
the female rain of the Pueblos and Navajos, when the rain is
feathery, and the horizon seems bright. Last night, a crescent
moon had drained through her own down-pointing tip.

    The last person I talked to was an Indian who was angry
at the proliferation of plastic shamans, both Anglo and Indian,
who took a bit of this and a bit of that, exploited a tradition
here, capitalized on a weakness there, and stuck the whole
mess on a kind of New Age sentimentality and desperation.
I was angry too, but I was thinking: Isn't this how many sects
and religions have gotten started? A bit of this, a bit of that,
arising at times of crisis and attracting all sorts of liminal types.
Lollards, Hutterites, Moravians, Waldensians … they have
been on my mind all day. The Albigensians took the New
Testament from Christianity, but rejected Christ's divinity,
the authority of bishops, saints and images. From Thracian
Orphism they took the doctrine of metempsychosis (Molly
Bloom's "met-him-pike-hoses." She too took what she wanted).
From Manichaeism they learned how to escape the kingdom of
Satan by foreswearing such pleasures as sex and war. Respect
was paid to women; pacifism was an ideal. Repudiating the
spirit of the Crusades, they were rewarded by one of their very

own. They were massacred when Simon de Montfort attacked them in 1209 with the Albigensian Crusade....

But they had descendants, literally and figuratively. My grandmother's family had Huguenot origins. She was from the wool country of Tilney St. Lawrence in northern Norfolk, where Huguenot weavers had settled after the Edict of Nantes cast out half a million Frenchmen from their homeland.

*

I am attracted to opposites: Catholicism's sensuality and mythic resonance, and Puritanism's abstract essence. The opposite of this attraction is repulsion, and I am repulsed by them too. But the need for sacralizing is strong, and gives rise to a life of irony, at once sacred and profane, for the sacred often has to be invented, or if rediscovered, it is a kind of reinvention, a Williamsburg of the soul.

It can sometimes be recreated in art, but no modern art has the power of Altamira or Les Trois Frères. Power is *there,* even for us, however vestigially. It doesn't have to be learned, even though we can never be sure of prehistoric (or "primitive") "meaning." Descriptions we were given did more harm than good, interpreting the living with dead nineteenth-century terminology ("magic," "fertility," "ancestor worship," "animal worship," and so on).

The modern cult of the primitive only goes back to the spring of 1906 when Picasso began *Les Demoiselles d'Avignon,* and visited the Trocadéro in Paris. Ethnological specimens and data on the process of evolution became aesthetically visible. In the process, objects were ripped from their original contexts, their powers aborted. They were placed in the context of our alienation. And now, at the dying end of the process, the cross-fertilization of art and ethnology has given us attenuated constructions such as Nancy Grimes' sticks, ropes, stones, shells, and dirt, which I saw at the MOMA "Primitivism" show a few years ago, just as earlier it had given us Frank Lloyd Wright's romantically fatuous hollyhock house. Wright's house appropriates, but it is clearly serious and unironic. Grimes' constructions, on the other hand, could be mistaken as satiric. Something has happened in the years between. Recently, anthropologists such as Clifford Geertz and James Clifford have noted the crisis, which might be termed epistemological, and endemic. Who is studying whom? "Who are now to be persuaded? Africans or Africanists? Americanists or American Indians?" (Geertz).

When the sacred infuses we forget the whole idea of art. The mythic and sacred is simultaneous and eternal. Nothing is erased. It accretes and grows, like the great hall at Pech-Merle or Les Trois Frères where animals are drawn on animals, over the years. The image has itself powers of renewal. Everything exists simultaneously on at least two planes, the largely visible world, and the often invisible world. Energy ("power") is the link, so even that which is "empty" (in this area, inverted commas alienate the text, shake up the words used—I am writing about the elusive unwriteable) is charged and reverberant, like the caves themselves. It is, in fact, the direct analog of the "empty" caves where the paintings were made, or performed, or the "empty" prairie or forest ("wilderness") where indigenous people lived their full existence. Luther Standing Bear tells of a Sioux child's education into the plenitude of the world: "But very early in life the child begins to realize that wisdom was all about and everywhere and that there were many things to know. There was no such thing as emptiness in the world.... Everywhere was life, visible and invisible."

The prehistoric synoptic essence of animal form left free as much as it incorporated. It combined freedom with necessity, almost like Zen painting (the powerful unpainted area in a Japanese painting is called *yonaku:* "white space"). Just as the structure of the band or group prevented coercion and promoted equality, so all directions have equal rights. (The animal paintings, as analyzed by Max Raphael, intuitively (?) utilized the principle of the golden section. The golden section would seem to be something of an absolute in the formal pleasure of human perception.)

In his book *Eskimo,* E.S. Carpenter notes that for an Aivilik an object he's working on has its own space; it doesn't have a special relationship with other objects. These objects "aren't meant to be set in place and viewed." Space is big enough for all to share. There is participation, not contemplation. So, with Ice Age paintings and their "principle of simultaneity," in the cave-dark we have a sharing of space and a participation in the meaning, the event-energy. In the dark, vision is limited. All the other senses come into play, senses that are stronger in an oral culture. As Walter J. Ong has pointed out, sound situates a man "in the middle of actuality and in simultaneity, whereas vision situates man in front of things and in sequentiality" (*The Presence of the Word*). This is a world filled, a world saturated with plenitude, unprioritized. Man simply has to participate. And since "spatial concepts are internalized action" (Piaget), our ancestors acted and thought in ways very different from us. (One can bet they were not like the characters in the once-popular "prehistoric novel"!)

The principle of simultaneity keeps nature intimate. It generates respect, this participatory timelessness that seems to come from the very caves of oneself. Our modern world dates from Plato's revolution in consciousness which made people separate themselves from their world; made them into a subject evaluating an object instead of "imitating" it. The "Homeric state of mind" ("oral," "archaic") was "something like a total state of mind" (Eric A. Havelock, *Preface to Plato*).

Brian Swann

Plato attacked the archaic pleasure-based, oral-grounded world of the poets and banished them from his republic, substituting for the poets' laden language that is experienced as it is understood (meaning saturated and saturating, the meaning one "stands under") an abstract language to describe and analyze experience. Thus begins the sad dualism of the West. But this idea of dualism, which for us spells isolation, strain, control, is for archaic societies part of the continuum, an everlasting unfolding. Duality, as Dennis Tedlock has said in *The Spoken Word and the Work of Interpretation,* is, in Mesoamerican thought (one might say in American aboriginal thought in general), "contemporaneous rather than sequential," complementary rather than oppositional. This has, of course, serious implications for "the problem of evil"!

How different all this is from our own traditions and principles of opposition and conflict, subordination, subjection, repression and subjectivity which, starting with Plato and gathering momentum with Descartes, have triumphed in our times with Marx and Freud! Marx imagined the "reconciliation" between man and nature will come when we see "nature becoming human," which is something like the end result of Hegelian idealism: brute materials tamed and cultivated. Freud saw nature as dangerous, something "projected," a kind of horrible emanation, something to be regulated. The principal task of culture, he says, is to "defend us against nature" and to increase our "power" (see Hans Peter Duerr, *Dreamtime,* page 315). However much Freud and Marx may have been qualified by thinkers and actors in recent years, most countries are still firmly committed to official policies of "growth" and exploitation.

The sacred should exist intimately, yet independent of us. But there is no numinous place left which we cannot destroy either with our banal curiosity or brutal assertiveness. We insist

206

on using everything. If only we'd listen to Thoreau: "This curious world we inhabit is more wonderful than convenient; more beautiful than it is useful; it is more to be admired and enjoyed than used." Yet shadows of the sacred can still touch us like a feather, and perhaps, at this late date, when the empyrean itself is cluttered with satellites, no more should be expected. For me, such shadows grow in quiet and solitude, the traditional conditions, becoming harder and harder to find. I am also beginning to find such shadows in science, which is not the traditional place, until one realizes that modern science is revealing a world as "mystical" as any master's or saint's.

*

I leave the warm room, its tang of rosemary which I'd sprinkled on the top of the stove to make incense. I pull on my hooded corduroy jacket, take the flashlight, and go out into the rain that has blackened and deepened. I walk past the fence that protects a garden shouldering into being. I run the flashlight over the seedlings. Some have been pushed out by rain or pulled out by wind. I plant them back in the black silt I'd hauled, bucket by bucket, from the old quarry, summer after summer. I'd spread it over slabs and chunks of bluestone that had been laid bare over the years, or worked their way up from below. I take some beans that have lost their grip, and weave their shoots through the chicken-wire fence. Holding the beam steady, I stare at leaf and bud, noting minute changes only obsession would note. I had put the tomatoes in too early. I bind those that have come off their sticks. I loop some pieces of cloth I found in my pocket into figures of eight, and tie. What light there is in the rain shivers against leaf and stem hairs. The globe wobbles, but the rain is unwavering.… The rain keeps you in the center, wherever you are. It calms the nerves. It is something you can count on.

There is a sound. I stand up. It could be geese returning. It could be the special sound of the rain … a bell, muffled, as if someone were taking care not to let it sound, like the bell in which Modomnoc carried bees when he crossed the pure-colored sea to Ireland, in a small boat from the east. I stare, and can make out the tree-stump on which I put leftovers for the raccoons. It looks human, trollish. Sometimes during the day it is covered with all sorts of birds pecking at the crumbs, opening and shutting their wings, so that from a distance it could be the figure of a goddess, like the picture I have on my desk of a prehistoric Anatolian Bird Goddess, each fat buttock an egg, whorls, spirals, and lines cut on the legs, perhaps ways of marking the season, or the years, or the Great Year, when the constellations sweep round the Pole Star…. *Ma* is the radical element in Indo-European, and maybe other languages. Even in Lakota, "mama" means a woman's breast. *Ma* is related to creativity and generation. "*Ma ganju*" means "rain." "*Mn-i*" is "water" (whence "Minnehaha"!) from "*ma*" + "*ni*," "life" or "breath." "*Maga*" is "garden," or cultivated field. It also means "goose," and "April" is "*maga agli wi,*" "the month when the geese return home," which is the month before planting in Sioux country.

There are scents, noises, objects…. I find it hard to go back inside. There is enough rain to make a new world. Swimming in my beam, a snail in his small ark. I remember an Irish snail riddle, which I learned for its sound, and whose references now elude me: "The pooka of the horns and the Tadha of the two watches." My mind slips gears. "Pooka" glides into "*pula*"…. Among the bushmen of the Kalahari "*pula*" means "rain." It also means "hello," and "money." Tomorrow I'll dig a trench to drain the garden. I'll lose everything otherwise.

Back in the house, rain is attracted to the lights. It smashes against the windows like flocks of tiny birds.

*

Next morning it is still raining. Rain slips off the ends of mulberry leaves like grease. I can sense beans sending out curling tentacles from underwater. Some will find nothing to grip, and curl over on themselves. Some will touch wire, and snap into action with a saving grasp. Others will climb up themselves, or, in mutual aid, bridge synapses inter-woven. They will bunch their delicate fingers—the whole group is a nerve until they flower, and then the fingers breathe.

I don't go out to dig a trench.

Think: Only five per cent of water on the globe is fresh, and seventy-five per cent of that is locked up in ice and snow. So we have available about one per cent, and ninety-nine per cent of that is groundwater at depths of up to one thousand feet....

I remember reading that someone a few hundred years back saw Indian corn hereabouts fourteen feet high.

I have a tendency to mope intellectually. I have to learn to see the ordinary. (Hui-neng: "The Tao is your ordinary mind.") Seeing is choice. If you examine eye movements you realize the image cast on the retina can never be the same because the eye is in constant motion. How to see as stationary that which is recorded on the retina as constantly moving? We *learn* to see, and then forget we've learned. We have to relearn in as unconscious a way as we learned. And then the mind will resonate, and make the world resonate, though the mind should be as if it had never resonated, and things should not remain in it.

*

There is a deer standing in the rain at the edge of what I call the lawn and which is, in fact, just a drained swampy area at the edge of the woods. While it stands, bone salts are depositing silently on pedicels, calcium is being pulled from the skeleton. He is growing antlers that are hot to the touch. No snow can melt on his coat for the hairs lose no heat. I have seen their eyes shine silver-white. I have seen the pupil turn green after death. He raises a foreleg and places it into a bed of moss, whose ancestors were tall as the white pines behind him, now girdled with rust blister.

The rain is relentless. It is a sad voice, the sad voice of all things extinct. It is Hannibal, whose city will soon be salt, riding the North African elephant, soon to disappear. Each drop is life. Even Darwin didn't know that fertilization could be accomplished with a single sperm.... If all men are brothers (and women sisters) how come half the world has blood which, if mixed with the blood of the other half, would clot it?

*

I pretend it is summer. I am down on my knees among the squash plants, and tomato bushes, inhaling their poison fragrance. Great yellow lamps of the squash throw yellow ceilings onto their leaves' undersides. My face is probably the color of pollen. The Chiricahua say the sun can stretch a net like a spider's and catch a person in it. They call the strands "sunbeams." If you damage them they will make a web inside you. If fear produces respect, if taboos mean care, I'm for both. Did you know:

The Chiricahua used to draw a charcoal ring around their anus and point it at the sky in order to bring out the sun?

St. Francis alternated strophes with a nightingale?

St. Kevin hatched a blackbird in his hand?

St. Dominic saw a chirping blackbird as a demon, caught it, plucked it alive, rejoicing all the while at the shrieks of the demon being exorcised?

*

The wind has joined the rain again. It is hurling down branches. One has fallen across the garden. If any birds have survived you'd never know it. We shall never see the sun again. I put another log on the fire.

*

Some shadows of the sacred:

The scanning electron microscope shows beautiful form dominating even tiny organism such as diatoms. Is this more proof of the argument for design?

An exact solution of Einstein's equation of general relativity, discovered by the New Zealand mathematician Roy Kerr, provided the absolutely exact representation of countless black holes spread throughout the universe before they were discovered. His revelation derived from a desire for the beautiful in mathematics. It found its exact replication in Nature. This would suggest that the mind responds most deeply to beauty. It would also suggest that the structure of the universe can best be phrased in terms of beauty and symmetry, however complex. There is certainly a large-scale structure to the seemingly random distribution of galaxies. Fractal geometry would tell us that the same structural principles inform large- and small-scale entities. The way of self-symmetry is shown in the way a broccoli floret's tiny bifurcations echo the branching of the stalk as a whole. To see eternity in a grain of sand is more than a poet's fancy. The way up and down are the same. Literally.

*

Hemoglobin may be as ubiquitous in plants as it is in animals, and be used for the same purpose: transportation of oxygen.

Hemoglobin has come down to us from a common ancestor of plants and animals.

The distinction between life and non-life might be artificial. They should be seen as lying on a continuum. On such a scale, a virus, which cannot duplicate on its own, would be somewhere near the middle. So would an ancient unknown proto-cell that became the ancestor of all life.

Some experts believe that growing crystals of clay formed the first replicating evolving systems and ushered in the age of organic cells.

The carbon atoms in our bodies (we are a carbon-based organism), have come floating down to us as carbon dioxide. They have been absorbed by the oceans, formed the plankton in those oceans, been buried in sediments that became rock, been buried in sediments that became oil…. They have been released back into the atmosphere through volcanoes, exhausts, chimneys, plants. The gold or silver in our teeth was created in a supernova explosion and expelled into space. We are stuff of the earth. We are stuff of the stars.

*

The quantum world is a world which I don't understand but which I'm delighted exists. It is a world of "unrealized tendencies for action" (Nick Herbert), not actual events; of tendencies on the move, but where nothing actually happens; where everything remains strictly in the realm of possibility.

*

The pheromone isobutyraldehyde, a middle-range fatty acid, characterizes the human female in mid-cycle. Its nearest relative in the carbon chain is the odor of bean sprouts. I love bean sprouts. Great champagne also has many aldehyde tones. I'm pretty partial to champagne, too. These fatty acids appear in the world's most delicious and expensive cheeses. Cheese is one of my favorite foods.

Ethyl alcohol has been detected in the giant gas clouds or clusters in our galaxy. Ethyl alcohol is vodka. Those clusters in the center contain enough vodka to fill more than 10,000 goblets the size of the earth.

The smallest sparrow has twice as many neckbones as the tallest giraffe.

*

I put another log on the fire.

Acknowledgements

American Voice: The Kiss.

Another Chicago Magazine: Lem.

Beloit Fiction Journal: Pol.

Caliban: Rain; A Man's; Winter Suite.

Fiction International: Tule Fog; Praxiteles; Whirligigs; The Clown in the Elevator, the Fool in the Machinery.

New Letters: A Small Bug.

Social Text: Cry the Beloved Country.

About the Author

BRIAN SWANN was born in Wallsend, England, in 1940. In 1963, he graduated as Foundation Scholar from Queens' College, Cambridge. He came to Princeton in 1964 as a Proctor Fellow, staying two years then leaving for Europe. He returned in 1968 as a Princeton National Fellow, earning a PhD in 1970, and becoming a U.S. citizen in 1980.

He has published many books in a number of genres, from poetry and fiction to children's books, from poetry in translation to Native American literature. He was founder and series editor of the Smithsonian Series of Studies in Native American Literatures and is founder and series editor of the University of Nebraska Press's Native Literatures of the Americas.

He has won a number of awards and prizes, including a National Endowment for the Arts fellowship in fiction, the John Florio Prize for the best Italian translation published in the UK, Italy's Premio Circe-Sabaudia and the Italo Calvino Award from Columbia University's Translation Center. In addition he won the University of Alabama Press Open Poetry Prize for *The Middle of the Journey,* the Ohio State University Press/The Journal Prize for *Autumn Road,* the Pleiades Press Lena-Miles Wever Todd Poetry Prize for *Snow House,* and the Autumn House Poetry Prize for *St. Francis and the Flies.* He has published other collections of poetry, such as *In Late Light* from Johns Hopkins University Press, and fiction such as *Dogs on the Roof* from MadHat Press.

His work has appeared in a number of scholarly journals, such as *English Literary History, Criticism, Novel, Nineteenth Century Fiction, English Miscellany,* and *Modern Poetry Studies,* as well as many anthologies and magazines, including *New Republic, The New Yorker, Paris Review, Hudson Review, American Scholar, Poetry,* and *Yale Review.* He has taught at Princeton and Rutgers and was director of the Bennington Writing Workshops. He is Professor of Humanities at the Cooper Union for the Advancement of Science and Art in New York City.

Other Works by Brian Swann

POETRY

The Whale's Scars (New Rivers Press, 1975).

Roots (New Rivers Press, 1976).

Living Time (Quarterly Review of Literature Contemporary Poetry Series, 1978).

Paradigms of Fire (Corycian Press, 1981).

The Middle of the Journey (University of Alabama Press, 1982).

Song of the Sky: Versions of Native American Songs (University of Massachusetts Press, 1993).

Wearing the Morning Star: Versions of Native American Song-poems (Random House, 1996).

Autumn Road (Ohio State University Press, 2005).

Snow House (Pleiades Press/LSU Press, 2006).

In Late Light (Johns Hopkins University Press, 2013).

St. Francis and the Flies (Autumn House Press, 2016).

Companions, Analogies (Sheep Meadow Press, 2016).

FICTION

The Runner (Carpenter Press, 1979).

Unreal Estate (Toothpaste Press/Coffee House Press, 1981).

Elizabeth (Penmaen Press, 1981).

Another Story (Adler Publishing Co., 1984).

The Plot of the Mice (Capra Press, 1986).

Dogs on the Roof (MadHat Press, 2016).

TRANSLATION

The Collected Poems of Lucio Piccolo, with Ruth Feldman (Princeton University Press, 1972).

Selected Poetry of Andrea Zanzotto, with Feldman (Princeton University Press, 1976).

Shema: Collected Poems of Primo Levi, with Feldman (Menard, 1975).

Collected Poems of Primo Levi, with Feldman (Faber and Faber, 1988).

The Dawn Is Always New: Selected Poems Of Rocco Scotellaro, with Feldman (Princeton University Press, 1979).

The Dry Air of the Fire: Selected Poems of Bartolo Cattafi, with Feldman (Ardis/Translation Press, 1981).

Primele Poeme / First Poems of Tristan Tzara, with Michael Impey (New Rivers Press, 1976).

Selected Poems of Tudor Arghezi, with Impey (Princeton University Press, 1976).

Currents and Trends: Italian Poetry Today, edited, with many translations, with Feldman (New Rivers Press, 1979).

Euripides' The Phoenician Women, translated with Peter Burian (Oxford University Press, 1981).

The Hands of the South: Selected Poems of Vittorio Bodini, with Feldman (Charioteer Press, 1981).

Rain One Step Away: Selected Poems of Milih Cevdat Anday, with Talat Halman (Charioteer Press, 1981).

Rome, Danger to Pedestrians, by Rafael Alberti (Quarterly Review of Literature Contemporary Poetry Series, 1984).

Garden of the Poor: Selected Poems of Rocco Scotellaro, with Feldman (Cross Cultural Communications, 1992).

CHILDREN'S BOOKS

The Tongue Dancing (Rowan Tree Press/Simon and Schuster, 1984).

The Fox and the Buffalo (Green Tiger Press, 1985).

A Basket Full of White Eggs (Orchard Books/Franklin Watts, 1988).

Turtle and the Race Around the Lake (Sierra Oaks Publishing, 1996).

The House With No Door: African Riddle-poems (Browndeer Press/Harcourt Brace, 1998).

Touching the Distance: Native American Riddle-poems (Browndeer Press/ Harcourt Brace, 1998).

EDITING

Smoothing the Ground: Essays on Native American Oral Literature (University of California Press, 1982).

Recovering the Word: Essays on Native American Literature, with Arnold Krupat (University of California Press, 1987).

I Tell You Now: Autobiographical Essays by Native American Writers, with Krupat (University of Nebraska Press, 1987).

Poetry from the Amicus Journal (Tioga Press, 1990).

On the Translation of Native American Literatures (Smithsonian Institution Press, 1992).

Coming to Light: Contemporary Translations of the Native Literatures of North America (Random House, 1995).

Native American Songs and Poems, An Anthology (Dover Publications, 1996).

Here First: Autobiographical Essays by Native American Writers, with Krupat (Modern Library, 2000).

Poetry Comes Up Where It Can: Poems from the Amicus Journal, *1990-2000* (University of Utah Press, 2000).

Voices From Four Directions: Contemporary Translations of the Native Literatures of North America (University of Nebraska Press, 2004).

Algonquian Spirit: Contemporary Translations of the Algonquian Literatures of North America (University of Nebraska Press, 2005).

Born in the Blood: On Translating Native American Literature (University of Nebraska Press, 2011).

Sky Loom: Native American Myth, Story Song (University of Nebraska Press, 2014).